EVENING TREATS

A Collection of Short Stories

Cheryl Russell

Contents

The Walk

The two men were walking along the road chatting. At the same time they were looking around them observing everything that was going on.

"I'm really not sure what to do," said Jason, the younger of the two.

"But if you're not happy…." replied Brian.

"I'm not but it's not that simple. I've got Sophie and the kids to consider."

Brian nodded in understanding.

There was a pause as Jason stopped abruptly and pointed to two teenagers in the children's playground. "They look as if they are up to no good."

Brian agreed so they rushed off over to the playground.

"Oi you," yelled Brian.

The two teenagers seeing the men turned and ran off dropping the bag. Jason was the first to reach it and picked it up. Looking inside he wrinkled his nose. The stench was overpowering. Inside was a pile of rotten, cracked eggs.

"Well what were they going to do with them?" asked Brian.

Jason shrugged and holding the bag away from him he rushed to the bin and disposed of it. "I suppose we won't need this for evidence," he said.

"Evidence of what? We don't even know what was going on before they ran off. They should have been in school anyway."

"Do you know them?"

Brian shook his head. "They don't ring a bell."

They continued their walk along the high street. Jason pulling his uniform straight which had become crumpled with running. He smoothed his hair back into place which was also askew. It didn't matter how hard he tried he still managed to look a mess which was the butt of jokes back at the station. Brian on the other hand continued looking pristine and smart. Brian felt sorry for Jason. He knew Jason wasn't happy and felt he was in the wrong job. Police work wasn't for everyone and it didn't suit Jason. The long hours and shift work caused arguments for Jason with Sophie who hadn't signed up for an absent husband.

Brian now said, "You'll have to make a decision soon you know. Sophie won't stand for this much longer. Don't forget I heard her on the phone to you. You'll have to choose the job or her."

Jason dropped on a nearby bench head in his hands. "I don't know what to do," he said in despair.

Brian sat silent not saying anything. He felt they had reached a crucial moment and Jason had to work it out for himself.

Jason shook his head from side to side. "It's too much. I'm so tired all the time. Getting up in the middle of the night to get to work isn't fun. I have to be so quiet so as not to wake the children. I can't go on like this. I need to leave but what will I do instead?"

"There are plenty of things you could do that would be more regular hours or you could go back to uni and study something else."

"But the police is all I've ever wanted to do, ever since they were so good after dad was murdered. No leaving isn't an option. If Sophie doesn't like it she'll have to leave. Decision made."

Knitting

I sat there on the chest of drawers, proud of my place at the front. Amelia loved me dearly and would always pick me up and handle me. It is true she had progressed since then but I was her first piece of knitting. Only a few rows but that was something special. Not only that but she had managed to include several different colours giving a rainbow effect, orange, blue, green and yellow. Her grandmother taught her how to knit and now it's a hobby she loves although she's only ten years old. She knitted me a couple of years ago and I still remain her favourite piece. She looks at me and handles me every day.

"Look grandma, I've still got it," cries Amelia next time she sees her grandparents. She proudly holds me aloft.

They look at me and nod, smiling happily. It doesn't matter that they have seen me hundreds of times they still react as if it is the first.

I have many adventures with Amelia as she takes me on holiday with her, claiming she can't sleep if I'm not there. I travel in her pocket. I went to France one year and enjoyed lazing on the beach in the South of France. I've been to Scotland as well but didn't enjoy that so much. France was much better as I didn't understand the language. It is true sounds were a bit muffled living in a pocket but I could hear enough to know it wasn't English. Scottish was a form of English. It seemed to be anyway although I couldn't understand what was said half the time. Amelia would take me out of her pocket and I was described as wee. Well that didn't impress me as I thought that was something you did on the toilet! I kept hearing wee in France as well but apparently that meant yes.

One day at home in my usual place the window was open and the wind blows me on to the floor and under the bed. It's dark and horrible. It has a horrible musty smell and the dust well, there is nothing I can say about that. Piles high of it, I feel as if I am drowning in it. Amelia was distraught when she arrived home from school and couldn't find me. Always on arriving home she would rush upstairs, stroke me and tell me all about her day. On this occasion I'm not there. I try calling out to her and telling her I am there but she doesn't hear me. She bursts into loud tears, bringing her mum rushing thinking something awful has happened, which of course it has, I wasn't there.

As expected Amelia can't sleep that night. She cries and cries, unable to believe she had lost me. Her mum suggests she knits something else and replace me but it seems that wasn't an option. It wouldn't be the same. It was a great relief to me of course as I thought I was irreplaceable as well. It breaks my heart not being able to let Amelia know where I am, that I'm safe still here for her.

The next day while Amelia was at school her mum has a good search of the room including moving the bed. It's with much relief I'm found I don't think I could have coped with being there much longer. Her mum gives me a good dust which is a welcome relief. The dust has been making me choke but that's over now and I'm placed back in my rightful place waiting for Amelia to come home again.

The Gift Voucher

Annalie had a £20 gift voucher and was on her way to spend it. She would going to her favourite shop and couldn't wait to reach it. If she could walk faster she would, but she was going as quickly as she could without breaking out into a trot. She took no notice of her surroundings, she stayed focused on her end goal.

On arrival she inhaled deeply and sighed. This was luxury, the rich smell of new books, which she loved so much. When at home she would often pick up a cherished book just to sniff it.

She made her way to her first choice, mysteries. She especially liked psychological thrillers. She loved trying to work out who did it and why. Laughing to herself at the thought as she was always wrong, but she took great pleasure in trying nevertheless. She wouldn't make a good detective she knew, but while it was only in a book she wasn't doing any harm.

Browsing she picked one book up after another. She was juggling a couple of books and her handbag, trying not to drop anything.

"You here again, Annalie," commented a member of staff.

She turned and grinned, "Of course, where else would I be when I have a gift voucher to spend."

"You are in so often you're a part of the furniture. I don't know how you manage to fit them all in at home."

"There's always room for a new book," she said, starting to laugh.

It was always a pleasure coming here, the staff were so friendly and helpful if she was looking for a particular book. Even if she wasn't buying she would come in to browse.

Her family tried to get her to buy a kindle but she always resisted. There was nothing like turning pages of a real book with an attractive cover. Yes, she acknowledged to herself there were advantages of a kindle such as hundreds of books that didn't take up any space but she was determined never to go down that route.

She made her decision and carried half a dozen over to the cash desk. She could never be content with one or two books, she always went for more, being unable to decide between them.

The Gift

Anna looked at her husband lying there, eyes closed and felt nothing. She was empty, devoid of all feeling. This had been the case for a while now. If she thought about it, she could track it down to three months ago when she had been going through a bad patch at work. At around the same time her mum had become seriously ill, also their new neighbours had turned out to be the neighbours from hell.

She suspected her husband of having an affair but hadn't any proof to confront him. He stayed later and later at the office and came home smelling of perfume. She was sure it was his new secretary. She needed to work out how to catch him.

Oh no, not again, the neighbours were hammering and drilling. It was only 6am. What could they be doing so early, but this was becoming a regular feature, sometimes they were at it all night. She was so tired. She envied her husband who managed to sleep through it all.

She got up and went downstairs, at least it would be less noisy. She knew she wouldn't sleep but at least it would help the headache hammering at her forehead.

Anna wished she could feel something. This emptiness inside was horrible. She used to love her job and Bill but now – she shrugged her shoulders. Maybe there was something wrong with her.

"Here you are!" said Bill, her husband walking into the living room where she was sitting.

She looked at him, giving him a weak smile.

"How long have you been sitting there?"

"Not long," she said, not wanting to get into a discussion.

It had been like this for a while. Bill would try making a conversation and she would cut him off. If he was having an affair maybe she couldn't blame him, she was pushing him away.

"Here you are," he said, holding out a package.

She opened it and found a new perfume. Suddenly the emptiness vanished and she voluntarily went into his arms and held on tight as if to stop herself from drowning. She felt secure again, all the problems were in her head, he loved her and that was all that mattered.

In the Quietness

She looked down the street, it was eerily quiet, so unusual. The absence of traffic noticeable. No cars or lorries roaring down this street. She longed for things to return to normal. Normal? Would it be again? She wasn't sure. Life stood still, frozen in time.

She could never have imagined what had been going on. It was a nightmare, the sort of thing that happened on television not in real life.

There was a crowd still gathered at the end of the street, silent, not talking. Stunned, unable to take in what had occurred. She walked towards the people and noticed the cameras. Reporters, like vultures were standing wanting their piece of flesh. It was just another story to them.

Suddenly anger took over, "What are you looking at? Let them rest in peace can't you! They should be allowed some tranquillity now they're dead. They certainly didn't get it near the end of their life."

The reporters turned to her. She had been the only voice shattering the silence of this deathly street. She didn't wait, she turned and walked away, tears streaming down her face.

How could such a thing have been allowed, undiscovered until now. It was right under their noses and they knew nothing of the horrors that had been going on in that house. Those poor children. They'd seemed a private, unassuming couple. It was unbelievable that they had been capable of such evil.

It was only yesterday the police had arrived after an anonymous tip off. They'd dug up the back garden and then the full extent of the cruelty was discovered. Ten bodies, children whose life had been snuffed out too early. The couple tortured and killed their own children and kidnapped others. It was impossible to comprehend what those poor children went through in their last hours of life. Death must have come as a merciful release.

She went back inside, shut the door, shaking her head.

Screaming into the silence

Claire opened her eyes, blackness all around her. Where was she? This didn't feel like her bedroom. She was laying on something hard, like concrete. She tried feeling around with her hands and found they wouldn't move. What was wrong with her? Why was it so quiet? She couldn't remember anything. The last thing she remembered was walking home from the party. She opened her mouth to scream. This brought a response.

"Shut up, you stupid cow," came a voice from far away.

She screamed again.

"If you don't shut up, I'll shut you up."

Very frightened, she wondered what was happening? A nightmare she would wake up from perhaps? She was sure she was awake though.

"Who are you?" she asked.

"It doesn't matter who I am," came the response. "I was asked to keep you quiet until Darren comes."

She gasped. Darren was her fiancé. What was this all about? Surely it must be a nightmare, she'll wake up and laugh about it with him.

"Why would Darren do this to me? We are supposed to be getting married next month."

There was a laugh from the other side of the door. "Darren get married? He is already married – to me!"

She was confused. Darren gay? He was pure blooded heterosexual. What did it all mean? Whatever was happening she knew she was in a lot of trouble. She tried screaming again.

"I warned you, since you can't keep quiet, I'll have to quieten you."

He bent down and put a rag over her mouth so she could no longer make a sound.

Meanwhile Darren was sleeping soundly, dreaming of the wedding next month. He couldn't wait to marry his girlfriend of two years. It had taken ages to get her to agree to taking things a step further. He had no idea what was happening to his beloved.

When he woke up he immediately phoned Claire which was the first thing he did every day. There was no answer which he thought was strange. They both enjoyed their first chat of the day.

Steve, his best man, smiled to himself as he saw the name appearing on the screen. There would be no wedding he would make certain of that. He hoped in the timescale he had to convince Darren that it wasn't Claire he loved but himself, Steve. Soon it would be time to take the plan to the next step. He would make himself invaluable to Darren during the panic and search for Claire. He would make sure Darren thought that she had just changed her mind. It would take time but he had all the time in the world.

The Letter

I'm Hattie and I'm writing this with my sister Hettie. We have a good life with our mum who loves us so much and spoils us rotten. The complaint we have is that she insists on cleaning our house regularly and she never puts things back as they should be. This means we have to get to work and rearrange things. Very annoying. I've discovered a great way to punish mum when she annoys us and disturbs our routine. A nicely bitten finger is great, it works a treat. She leaves us alone then. We love the games she plays with us, but she always makes sure we go back to bed before we're ready so we have to capture her attention again. She always lets us have our own way and she picks us back up again.

We probably should say at this point that we are gerbils and she is crazy about us. I'm the dominant one. We're very close to each other and if I sleep somewhere different I know Hettie will come and sit next to me to make sure I'm ok.

I have a lot of problems with my teeth. Mum has to take me to the animal doctor which I hate but I always get some porridge to eat afterwards, it's made with water as milk isn't good for us.

I gave mum a fright once as she couldn't see me, she thought I had escaped but I was there. Unfortunately, she disturbed my sleep by trying to find me. I really don't know what her problem was. I had decided to sleep under an egg box. It seemed perfectly normal to me but she thought I should be found in the nest we had built for ourselves. She found it hysterically funny when I moved the egg box.

We like to think up different things to cause a bit of mischief and then we just stand up tall, sniffing the air so she forgives us instantly. She is so silly we just have to look particularly cute and she will let us get away with murder.

We want to say how much we love her as well. We know we are lucky to have her as our mum.

Hattie and Hettie.

Instant Connection

Maddie sat on the park bench munching on her cheese and tomato sandwich. It was a quiet day for a change, nothing happening. Usually on a nice day like today there would be a lot of young children playing with harassed looking mothers. Dog walkers out for their stroll. The dogs were a pain though as they would approach her wanting to smell the lunch she was eating.

Someone approached her and sat down at the other end of the bench. She glanced across at him curiously. He looked about her age, black hair, smartly dressed with glasses. The frames made him look quite attractive. She looked at him with more interest. She gave him a shy smile when he glanced across.

"Hello," he said, in a deep voice.

She responded with a hello of her own.

He moved along the bench to sit beside her. Opening a packet of crisps he offered her one which she took with a polite thank you.

He introduced himself as Michael. They shook hands, both giving a shy smile.

"Do you come here often," he asked in that lovely deep voice of his.

"Every day for lunch," she said.

They continued chatting, each feeling an instant connection with the other. When they had finished eating and it was time to go their separate ways they stood and shook hands politely. They agreed to meet same place, same time the next day.

This became their routine for the next few months. Michael, decided to take the next step and ask her out on a proper date. Maddie was quick to accept as this was what she had dreamed about for the few months they had been meeting and chatting. They had so much in common. They both enjoyed the romantic comedy they went to see and soon became regulars at the cinema. There was always something they wanted to see and as they had the same taste in films they enjoyed them as much as each others company.

It wasn't long before they started talking of settling down together.

A year after they met they were married and looking forward to a life of blissful happiness.

It Came in the Mail

Shelley held the parcel at arms length and eyed it warily. She took it through to the living room, placing it on the glass coffee table. She looked at it sat there. She didn't dare touch it. So many such parcels had been delivered recently and their contents were never nice. One such occasion had been a dead rat with a note attached warning that she would be next. The police had been unwilling to do anything, but what could they do anyway? She had no idea who could be sending them to her. As far as she knew she had no enemies. Why would anyone target her anyway? Just thirty years old she worked as secretary in a doctors surgery a few minutes from where she lived. She had a lovely boyfriend whom she had been seeing for about a year now. They were talking about getting married but so far had done nothing but speak of it.

Her boyfriend thought she was being overly sensitive, convinced she was making something out of nothing. She couldn't make him understand how frightened she actually was. Quite spooked by them they were causing nightmares at night. She would wake up screaming which really annoyed Jonathan her boyfriend. He was staying over less often these days, fed up with the disturbed nights. This had been going on for a month now. He kept telling her she needed to get a grip but that didn't help. How she wished he would help her find out who was doing this, but he just laughed it off. The parcels were practical jokes to him, nothing more nothing less.

She decided to leave this one for him to open when he came round. She fully expected something to happen anytime. He turned up during the evening, later than normal. When he walked in she sighed with relief. Now the parcel could be opened.

He didn't even kiss her before saying, "I see you've had another one then."

She nodded unable to speak. On asking what it contained she just shrugged. Irritated he grabbed the box and ripped it open. She drew back in horror as she saw him lift a gun out.

He laughed as he handled it, warning her that something was very wrong here.

He pointed the gun at her, his finger on the trigger.

"What do you think you're doing? Put that thing down, it might go off."

Still he held it, ignoring her. Suddenly things clicked into place and she gasped. "It was you, wasn't it?"

"Finally, you've worked it out," he sneered.

"But why? You're supposed to be my boyfriend."

"That's what I wanted you to think. Remember Carrie?"

She shrank back at the name. Carrie had been her best friend until she died in a car accident.

"I see you get it now. It was your fault," he said, before pulling the trigger.

Trouble in Paradise

They looked at each other, shaking their heads. It wasn't going to work at all. They were trying to book a holiday but were having problems with the dates. They had worked out when they could both be off, but the dates they wanted were all booked. It seemed hopeless. They decided to try another travel agent. Again, they had no success.

"You know we should try it online, we might have more options that way."

"Good point, let's look this evening."

Switching on the laptop they went to search for something.

"Hey this looks good. There's a pool which would be wonderful for you, you could have your early morning swim you are so fond of."

She smiled. That would be blissful. She loved her early morning swim. She always got up early so she could go for a swim before work. Keeping it up on holiday would be great. She looked over his shoulder and sighed. If only they could get that hotel they'd be in heaven. The pool looked so blue, the same colour as the sky. She'd enjoy the water and the sun shining brightly. They managed to book it without any problem. This decided them. In the future they would go straight online and try to book direct to avoid travel agents and the problems with them that they had encountered this time.

The Missing Piece

She opened her eyes and looked around feeling disorientated and confused. Where was she? Who was she? She tried getting up to look for a mirror, that might give her some more clues. She realised she was in a bed. Getting out of bed proved to be a challenge as her legs wouldn't support her. She started to feel frightened, what had happened? Looking around the room she discovered it was bare except for the bed and a chair next to it.

The door opened and James walked in. "You're awake then."

She nodded and asked, "Who am I? Where am I? Why can't I remember anything?"

"You have been in a nasty car accident that caused significant trauma to your brain. We are hopeful your memory will start to come back bit by bit. In the meantime you are safe with us. You are in a specialist rehab centre where we deal with complex issues like yours. We don't know your name as you haven't been able to remember anything. There have been no queries for a missing person matching your description. We are currently calling you Jenny."

Jenny sat quietly not knowing what else to say. This was all too much and very frightening.

"Are you feeling up to a chat now? I'm James, a psychologist here. We have been having chats over the past few days, but we are no nearer to working out who you are."

Jenny thought this all a bit odd. She even wondered if James was who he said he was. For some reason that she couldn't identify she felt she had to be very careful, not knowing who to trust. There were alarm bells ringing in her mind but she didn't know why. If only she could somehow find that elusive memory it would help. Suddenly a name popped into her mind, Clare. Was that her name she wondered.

"Was anyone else involved in the car accident?" she asked.

There was a slight hesitation before James answered, "We don't have any details here."

This didn't ring true in her mind especially as she had noticed the hesitation. She would have to tread carefully if she was to get any information about what happened.

"I seem to remember the name Clare," she said warily, wanting to sound him out.

"Do you think that is your name?" he asked eagerly. A little too much Jenny thought.

She shrugged not being able to answer that.

When James left she kept turning the name Clare over in her mind, sure there was something about the name. Suddenly it came to her, Clare was her teenage daughter. She was sure of it. That was a start anyway, at least something had come back to her. Now she needed to work out if Clare had been in the car with her and what had actually happened.

It was later that something else occurred to her. She remembered going downhill when suddenly the breaks failed on her car. She remembered another car travelling in the other direction, she tried slowing down but couldn't. She tried weaving the car from side to side in an effort to slow her speed down but to no avail. The inevitable happened and she crashed head on with the other car. She knew she had been in a hurry and Clare had been in the car with her. Her name she now remembered as being Esther.

Suddenly memories started coming back into her mind. Her husband was known to outbursts of temper towards her and Clare. She had been leaving him and had planned it for days prior to this. He had been getting worse and had been known to make death threats. Could he be behind this? Was Clare all right?

James popped his head around the door later. Noticing how distraught she looked he entered. "You've remembered?" he asked.

"I was leaving my violent husband. My daughter Clare was in the car. Is she all right?"

"Oh Esther my darling, how could you think that you were leaving me? Do you really think I would allow that?"

Esther gasped, "You're my husband?"

He nodded before lifting a pillow and putting it over her face.

Revenge

He ran without looking back. He didn't want to see the result of his handiwork. The flames were roaring now as the fire took hold. He could hear screams but didn't turn, he hoped they wouldn't escape in time. After what they did to him, they deserved all they got.

Sharon and Dave had been his foster parents. His social worker had told him they were good people, insisting that he was safe now. They didn't have a clue what it was like. He had been put through too much, starting when he cried out in nightmares from his troubled past. Instead of comforting him they threatened to do all sorts if he woke them up again. When he wet the bed they refused to change bedding, making him sleep in urine soaked sheets. The smell made him retch but he tried to avoid being sick, not wanting to cause further trouble to fall on his head.

He wished he knew what to do because social services wouldn't believe him as they were supposed to be wonderful foster parents able to cope with anything. Huh, he thought, he didn't see much evidence of that. The tiniest thing and he would be locked in the small cupboard under the stairs. Sharon and Dave were just like his parents. On one occasion he was shut in the garage over night for disturbing them with yet another nightmare. He was made to lay on the concrete floor and sleep. No mattress or pillows. Nothing to cover him either. He lay there shivering as it was a freezing cold night. There would certainly be a frost the next day. He didn't know which was worse the garage or the cupboard. The cupboard only gave him enough room to sit hunched up, but at least he could lay down in the garage.

It was hard when there was nothing to prove what he was going through. There were no bruises as they didn't touch him physically, they didn't need to they had other ways of getting at him. Whenever his social worker paid a visit they were on their best behaviour. Pleasant, caring people who would do anything for him. He didn't know how they could get away with it. Any attempt at telling the truth always met with disbelief, convinced he was getting them muddled up with his parents.

He wanted revenge on those who had hurt him but knew he had to bide his time. If anything were to happen while he was still there suspicion might fall on him. Bitterness and hatred built up inside him and the longer he kept it to himself the worse it got.

If only he could get away, escape, but where would he go? He didn't relish being on the streets it would be as bad as living with the Duncan's.

He tried keeping out of trouble, being quiet and only speaking when directly spoken to. This seemed to anger them as well, but if he talked they would be worse towards him so he couldn't win. He'd no idea what they wanted as everything was wrong. He felt he even had to have permission to breathe!

He stayed there until he was sixteen when his social worker helped him get a flat of his own. It was during this time he started thinking about revenge. All those feelings that had built up inside him needed an outlet. He waited though, not wanting to do anything too soon so it wouldn't be pinned on him. He started in small ways getting into practice for when the time came. Cars were a good target. The mysterious spate of fires were never solved. He was getting away with everything. He wasn't getting any satisfaction or release from the pent up feelings though. He needed to get back at Sharon and Dave for that.   By the time Darren was ready to get his revenge he was twenty one. If he was careful no one would ever realise it was him as he had waited so long.

....

He continued running, ensuring no one would see him and place him at the scene. It was the next morning when he saw it in the paper. Oh no, he had slipped up. He hadn't done his research, the family who died in the fire were not the Duncan's, they must have moved in the intervening years. He kicked himself, how could he have been so stupid as to make such an assumption. It was over and he could do nothing about it.

What it means to lose

It was that part of the day Ellie dreaded most. They were supposed to be picking teams for netball. She knew the captains would never choose her. She was always last, hopeless at any type of sport. She couldn't blame them really that is how she felt about herself. She was just a loser. Going through the entire day without anyone speaking to her was excruciatingly difficult. How she wished she could avoid school altogether. If only someone would speak to her. Why did everyone see her as such a loser? She knew they whispered about her behind her back. Sometimes the boys would call out names or ask her out but it was never meant in a nice way. Sometimes someone would stick a leg or bag out to trip her up when she passed. She felt so alone and no one cared or noticed what she went through.

Ellie would go home at the end of the day and hide in her room so no one in her family would see her tears. Tears that spoke of much suffering and torment. Did anyone really care? She looked at her bare arms that told a story of their own. Scratch marks all down both arms telling of the extreme distress she felt.

There were times when she wanted to crawl into a hole and hide away forever. To leave this world behind, that would feel so good. No one knew exactly what was happening and how she felt because she kept it well hidden behind a smile. There were occasions when she would like to confide in someone, but not her parents, they were too disinterested. They would dismiss it and then she would hurt even more. Even her parents thought Ellie was a loser, or they would have been more interested in what was happening to her.

There was only one solution, one way out. Once she was gone maybe they would understand what she went through, what it felt like to be a loser all the time.

My Followers

I closed the front door with a sigh of relief. My whole body slid down the door on to the patterned carpet. Who could it have been and why? I was so sure I was being followed but couldn't work out why anyone would want to. It was a mystery and it wasn't the first time either. It was only celebrities that had stalkers not an ordinary average person like me.

I phoned the police but as expected they weren't interested because no one had made an attempt to harm me in any way. I should let them know if any action was taken against me by the alleged stalker. They didn't even believe someone was following me, they thought it was a coincidence and someone else was walking the same route.

I shut the curtains not feeling at all safe. I didn't want anyone to look in through the window and see me. I shivered and made myself a hot drink with plenty of sugar. I remembered reading somewhere that it was good for shock. I didn't feel like eating.

I had a disturbed night with one nightmare after another about people coming after me. I terrified myself after one such dream by sitting bolt upright with a scream. It really looked as if there was someone in my room. I put the light on but saw no one. I listened hard trying to detect if there was someone in the flat, I couldn't hear even the tiniest creak. Getting out of bed I went to investigate. There was no one in the flat. I even looked behind the sofa to check for intruders that may be hiding.

I went to work as usual, wanting to keep things normal. Besides I would not achieve anything by staying at home. Everyone commented on how washed out I was and suggested I go home but I insisted on seeing the day through. I was probably safer at work than at home. At least at work I was surrounded by people.

I dreaded the walk home that evening. All to soon the day ended and I began the journey home. I kept sneaking glances behind me, trying to work out if anyone was there. I gasped as I noticed a shadow duck quickly into an alleyway when I turned my head to look behind me.

I retraced my steps determined to confront my follower. I was surprised to find myself coming face to face with a young woman.

"What do you want? You've been following me," I said bluntly, not in the mood to be polite.

"I – I think you maybe my mother."

There was a silence between us, I was stunned. This was the last thing I expected.

"Are you ok?" asked the young woman.

The colour had drained from my face and everything had started going black. She grabbed my arm and lowered me to the ground quickly. She took hold of my wrist to feel my pulse.

"It's ok," she said reassuringly. "I'm a medical student."

"What makes you think I might be your mother?"

"I was given my adoption papers by my parents. They gave your name as Amelia Long. That is your name isn't it?" she asked with a sudden note of caution in her voice.

I nodded unable to speak. Tears pricked my eyes and slid unchecked down my cheeks. It had all been so long ago now, but I remembered it as if it was yesterday. The baby had been taken away straight after the birth. I was too tired to argue with my mother who was absolutely convinced I could not keep her. I could see the disappointment in her eyes when she realised I was pregnant at such a young age. She should have protected me from the monster who had got me pregnant. She blamed me of course, refusing to believe her husband could do such a thing to his own daughter.

A day hadn't gone by when I wondered what had become of my little girl and now I knew, she was standing before me.

My Own Reflection

Jayne looked in the mirror through squinted eyes. She didn't want to see, yet was being drawn to look at herself. She hated mirrors they always made her seem fat.

She was a very thin young woman but the mirror distorted her body making her look enormous. She looked almost anorexic in reality but wasn't. She ate a lot, having a good, healthy appetite but never seemed to put on weight.

She opened her eyes properly to get a glimpse of herself. This time the mirror gave a very strange reflection, she was all curves and it looked as if there were two people there. What was it about this mirror? It must hate her. Deciding to look in another mirror she thought it would be best to go to town. She would try on some new clothes then she could look at her reflection in a proper mirror. A mirror that didn't have feelings, that was an inanimate object.

Jayne entered Marks and Spencers and looked around, grabbing a shirt and pair of trousers she took them to the fitting rooms. She hastily got her clothes off and looked in the mirror. She gasped, this mirror was the same. In fact, looking in it made her even more distorted. She really didn't know what to do. What was wrong with these mirrors? She saw a person appear behind her in the mirror. She turned in time to see a shadow disappear. She started to shake, not understanding what was happening and starting to feel frightened. She spoke quietly to the shadow to ask who it was.

In response the shadow grabbed hold of her and said, "I have been told to come and collect you. You do not belong to them but are one of us that is why you think the mirror is distorting your body. This happens to our kind which is why we don't have mirrors where I come from."

She allowed the shadow to take her hand and relinquished herself to it.

Letter to the Sea

She sat there, frowning, lips drawn in a straight line. Picking up the pen she began to write. The words just came to her as the pen flew across the page, trying to keep up with her racing brain. There was so much to write. She paused, looking at the stack of letters she'd already written. When she finished this one she would take them and deliver them.

The letters were addressed to her daughter whom she missed so much. She couldn't even put into words how much she missed her. Soon after the incident her husband walked out on her, leaving her alone. She had sunk into depression for ages afterwards before a therapist had suggested she write letters to her daughter. She would tell her how much she missed her, missed their shopping trips into town where they would always end up laughing at their different tastes.

They had been so close, yet when it came down to it, Amy realised how little she had known about what was going on in her daughter's life. Her eyes filled with tears as she continued writing. She longed to make her favourite meal, that they would have sat in front of the television, laughing at their favourite sitcom.

Letter finished Amy stood up and put the bundle in her bag. Getting in the car she drove the short distance to the sea. Parking the car she walked purposefully to the edge. She got the letters out and dropped them into the clear blue water. She watched them disappear, carried away by the water lapping the shore.

She said goodbye and went back to the car, tears streaming down her face. It had been two years since her daughter had been taken from her by the cruel sea. All she had left was a suicide note.

Now or Never

Eileen looked across the classroom wanting to steal a look at David. She thought he was hot, although no one knew it, not even her best friend Jane. She had kept her feelings to herself for the couple of months David had been at the school.

"I noticed you stealing a look at David," said Jane later.

Eileen blushed, unable to keep the colour from flooding her face.

"Oh my God, you like him don't you?" cried Jane.

"Shh," said Eileen. "Don't tell anyone please."

"Why didn't you tell me?"

"I didn't want anyone to know."

They stopped talking and hurried to the next lesson, but Jane hadn't forgotten and brought the subject up again at lunch time.

"Why don't you let me try and sus out how he feels about you. Maybe he returns the feeling."

"Don't you dare!" exclaimed Eileen completely mortified at the thought.

"How are you going to know if we don't do something? Unless you want to go up to him and ask him out."

"I couldn't do that!" Eileen was horrified at the thought.

"It's now or never," said Jane, for David was approaching, his eyes fixed on Eileen.

He opened his mouth to speak but struggled to get the words out.

"Well," said Jane. "You two need your heads banging together. Why don't you just ask her out and get it over with."

"Jane!" gasped Eileen at her friend's audacity.

"She's got a point. I did come to ask you to go to the cinema with me on Saturday."

"Really. I would love to," responded Eileen with a shy smile.

Full House

They all stood clustered around, nervously awaiting the start. Some were chatting, others twirling their hair around their fingers. Some chewing their nails. One brave girl went forward to peer through the closed curtain. She pulled back quickly before anyone would notice what she'd done. It was strictly forbidden for any of them to look. She moved back to the group.

"It's full up out there. It looks as if all seats have been taken."

"I suppose that's a good thing," said one of the others, not looking at all convinced.

"Five minutes girls," said their teacher.

"I need the loo," said someone quietly. This came as no surprise to any of them. She was always like that at every performance. No one really understood why she kept on attending dance lessons because she hated being involved in their performances.

"Right take your place girls, and good luck," said their teacher.

The girls rushed to take their place behind the curtain waiting for it to open and the music to start. The nervous energy they had felt disappeared.

The curtains opened and the opening music started. The girls started their energetic performance with lots of twirls and jumps. They skipped lightly across the stage, doing what they loved. It was hard work but this was the highlight of every term when they had the chance to perform in front of an audience. The tickets this time were completely sold out, so they had known it was going to be a full house.

Their moves could not be faulted, their performance flawless. They executed every movement gracefully, appearing to just fly through the air as they skipped and jumped about.

It was exhilarating to watch as well as to take part. The parents watched proudly and were vigorous with their applause at the end of each dance.

Some of the best dancers had solos which they carried off with ease.

Soon the evening was over and flushed faces of the girls sighed with relief, tired at the end of a long evening. They had enjoyed it as always but were ready for a hot bath and bed.

The Dream Dissolves

Marian wouldn't give up, she just wouldn't. The tears poured down her cheeks unchecked. All her life she'd wanted to be an actor, taking part in drama outside of school and going on to do theatre studies at drama school.

She'd finally been invited to try out for a part playing a major character in a soap opera on TV. Up until this moment she'd been playing minor roles in adverts. This was her dream to appear on television in a major programme. She thought she had performed well but still had been turned down. It was just a standard rejection with no criticism of her performance but it still hurt. Marian was crushed. Her dreams in tatters.

Her agent had phoned her with the news, he had been encouraging saying there would be other parts but she had put the phone down on him mid sentence. She didn't want to speak to anyone.

Marian had promised to ring her parents as soon as she heard anything, but couldn't bear to. She didn't want to hear the disappointment in their voices. They had been very supportive of her choice of career but of late had started making suggestions that she should try something else. Get a regular job and join an amateur dramatics group to pursue her hobby. She had been furious, hobby, was that all they saw it as? With the latest setback part of her wondered if they were right and she didn't have what it takes to succeed in this business.

What else could she do, she wondered. She wasn't qualified in any other area. She had put everything into improving her acting skills. She could type, but only slowly, so secretarial work was out of the question.

Deep in her head she still had the longing to be an actor and desperately hoped her agent was right that she would get a good part soon.

The phone rang but she ignored it, not wanted to talk to anyone. The answerphone took the call. She listened to the message, it was her agent offering the opportunity to be in yet another advert. She kept quiet, not quite being able to accept this anymore. If she was to act she wanted to do it properly, not just bit parts.

She sunk into depression, slipping off the radar for a good couple of months. The calls from her agent kept coming but Marian ignored them. In fact she ignored everyone. She was getting worried calls from her parents but she didn't get back to them.

She awoke one morning feeling motivated again, wanting to get out there and give every opportunity her best shot. On phoning her agent he heard there was a major opportunity in a drama series, taking down the details excitement began to build inside. This was what she was meant to do and she would succeed however long it took. Destiny was calling and acting was her destiny, her dream.

Uphill

Her whole body tensed up, she could feel the anxiety rising, nausea rose in her throat making her feel as if she was being strangled. Could she really do this? Everyone else believed in her but she had her doubts. No choice, it had to be done or she would feel a failure forever. She was sweating despite temperatures being sub zero, anxiety again. She had to do this to prove to herself she was perfectly capable. She would never forgive herself if she couldn't. The sky was blue and the sun shone brightly, dazzling the brilliant whiteness of the snow. She had on sunglasses to protect herself from the glare that leapt up at her. Her skis were on and she was ready to go. She glanced with great trepidation where she was supposed to ski. She was terrified, as she noticed it seemed to be a sheer drop down, no gentle slope for her. She wished herself anywhere else but where she was. What made her come back year after year for she only tortured herself? She traversed the slope but as she tried to make the turn anxiety tore at her again, she couldn't do it. Sitting down, she turned herself around ready to go back across the slope. Standing up again she made her slow way across. It was pointed out to her that she not only wasn't any lower down the slope but in actual fact had been skiing uphill. Not bad, she thought, at least she would remember this incident. Everyone else skied downhill but as usual she had to be different and ski uphill! Well it was an achievement of sorts if not the usual type. She refused to see it as a negative thing. It had to be positive. Everyone else raced past at high speed while she made her very slow way down the same way as she had started, sitting to turn round, sure she would lose control and have a nasty fall. She had been told she had plenty of restraint it was just confidence she lacked. She wasn't sure about that. Maybe skiing wasn't really her thing, she acknowledged, but she loved the snow covered mountains and the freezing temperatures. It looked so beautiful and undisturbed. How could anyone not love this. She loved mountains at any time of year. In the summer they would be a lush green, vibrant and alive. She sighed, what a privilege to be in these captivating surroundings. She continued skiing, eventually reaching the bottom and ready for a drink. She felt proud of herself as she looked up, seeing what she had accomplished even if it was in an unusual way.

Hope

She turned round, catching sight of her boss stood in the doorway watching her.

"Did you want something?" she asked.

He shrugged, not knowing what to say. In reality he had been enjoying the sight of her as she typed away at her computer. Her long, brown, silky hair with blonde highlights was an appealing vision before him, as was her black trouser suit she was wearing. She always looked smart for her job as secretary in a solicitors office.

James tried not to let it show how much he fancied Emily for he believed strongly in keeping things professional. He had the hope though that one day she might return his feelings. If only he knew what she felt, it would help, but he didn't see how he would ever know.

His partner Oliver knew how he felt after seeing him watching Emily for long periods and the quick glances he always gave her. Oliver didn't have the same qualms as James and didn't understand why James wouldn't ask her out. Oliver had a bit of a reputation as a womaniser, was always seen with a different girlfriend, but James wasn't like that, he was more cautious and unsure of himself around women.

Today though, James decided to try asking her out. He had hope that she would agree to lunch with him. That was all, there didn't have to be commitment to a relationship, just a simple meal to see how it went.

Emily was quick to accept the invitation having felt the same way about James.

Born Again

The phone call came, directing Geoffrey to wait outside at midnight. Now there was the difficulty of getting out without his parents hearing him. He went to bed at the usual time but was determined not to sleep. He had to pretend to be asleep, however, as his parents always looked in before going to bed themselves. He waited with excitement mounting for the time to come, he hadn't even put pyjamas on so all he would have to do was slip outside.

It was almost time to go. He got up quietly and started down the stairs, careful to avoid the creaky ones. The last thing he wanted was to alert his parents as this was a very important meeting that just couldn't be missed.

Outside Geoffrey crouched behind the bush in the front garden. It wouldn't do to be seen until they came for him.

Suddenly a whooshing noise could be heard, deafening him. He put his hands over his ears until the noise stopped. Standing up he walked towards the aircraft that had stopped in the street. A small hatch opened and a figure emerged.

"Hello Geoffrey," said a deep voice with a strange accent.

"Hi," replied Geoffrey in a small voice, slightly overawed by what was happening.

"Are you ready to join us?" queried the voice.

Geoffrey nodded unable to speak. He boldly walked over to the spaceship and climbed in.

"Before we go we have to go over a few things. Firstly you realise you will never come back don't you? We are your parents now and will guide and teach you how to survive as a Zogger. Our planet is much different to earth."

"I'm really excited and am looking forward to it. Ever since I first found out I was a secret Zogger who had been sent here to find out about the planet and teach you so you could stage a takeover."

"Your Zogger name is Goft so you need to remember that as that is what you will be called when we get back.

Goft nodded, that was an easy name to remember. He was looking forward to getting back to Zog so he could teach the people about planet earth. He was also looking forward to making acquaintance with his people again. He wouldn't miss his earthly parents as he had never allowed himself to become attached to them, knowing he was only there for a short period of time.

There was another loud noise as the spaceship took off with a loud roar, transporting its occupants to the planet Zog.

The Supervisor

The buzzer sounded. A static voice came over the intercom, "Number nine please immediately."

Someone stood up and walked on his hands out of the room. Everyone else breathed a sigh of relief, at least it wasn't them. It was always bad news to receive such a summons to the big boss, known only as K.

No one ever returned after seeing K and no one knew what he was like. Generally everyone looked alike with three eyes and three ears. The third eye was in the back of their heads and the third ear was on top. It was generally thought that K had horns as well, but remained unconfirmed. To see him meant banishment from the planet Zig.

They were all getting on with their work on the production line when in walked Zigzag. Stopping work they clustered around him, firing questions at him. "What does K look like? We didn't think we would see you again. What did he want?"

"Ok, ok, slow down and I'll tell you. Firstly I didn't see K! I was sent to an empty room that I've never seen before. This voice came through the ceiling asking me if I wanted to be made up to supervisor, reporting to one of K's minions. I wasn't given the option to refuse, it was pretty much dictated to me."

"What do you have to do?"

"It seems I'm a sort of spy. Sending back any information on any of our tribe who doesn't obey rules or anyone that dares to mention K at all. There's will be a huge crackdown on this.

Anyone found to be doing this will be banished from the planet with immediate effect. K feels there is a faction trying to usurp his leadership."

Zigzag suddenly found himself alone as the others slid rapidly away walking on their hands as all members of Zig did. No one wanted to be left with him, not wanting to be denounced. What no one knew and this included Zigzag was that he was suspected of heading a group trying to take over the planet. This was a test to see where his true loyalties lay.

Zigzag was equally determined that he would not report anyone. K was right he was in a special group of a select few who were fed up with K's dictatorial regime. He knew he would have to be extra careful not to alert the special leaf (the planets alien police) who would be quick to inform anything amiss. As a supervisor if caught for breaking rules he would have his hands and feet removed and if it was deemed to be a bad enough crime his eyes and ears as well. This would be done in front of all on the planet as a warning of what could happen to them.

....

Zigzag was worried. He knew they would be expecting him to give someone up but he couldn't do that. All he could think of was to pass information over to the faction wanting to depose K from his position of power. The only way they communicated was to leave breaths in the cubicle. Each breath would communicate a written message. It would be done in code just in case anyone else happened to come across it. Going into the office he glanced around making sure no eyes were poking out anywhere. You never knew with the special leaf they sometimes left eyes in place to spy on the people of Zig. Certain he was safe he started to breathe on to the board. Two breaths then pause, five rapid breaths then pause, three long breaths then stop. He placed the board in the agreed place then he quickly left the cubicle. He knew someone would be in touch soon, through the same method.

It wasn't long before a message came through. They thought he was in the best position to get information about K and his minions to them and were very encouraging of his new role. The only advice was to be careful as he would be closely watched to make sure he was above board.

He went off making sure eyes and ears were not watching and listening.

It was the next day that he started getting an inkling that something wasn't right. His third eye didn't seem to be working properly and he was having the same problem with his third ear.

What was he to do? Suspicions were in his thoughts that it might be the Special Leaf doing something to test him. Such problems did arise as a test to see what he would do and now as a supervisor he was in their radar.

He left a message for his leader in the faction for advice before contacting the Special Leaf. He got an immediate response saying to report it as it could be some sort of initiation technique.

He went to the Special Leaf cubicle and left them a message and went back to the production line. The summons came later. He went to room nine with much trepidation. A voice came through the recorded system wanting to test his eye and ear. He was offered a replacement straightaway.

Pleasantly surprised he slotted the eye and ear into place and went on his way. He started noticing that this new eye and ear was distorting things for him which made functioning more difficult. Everything appeared so large and all sound was magnified. It was quite frightening if he was honest. Contacting his faction the reply back was worrying. They were suggesting he needed to escape immediately because it sounded as if K was suspicious of where his true loyalties lay.

He hastily tried to make plans to get away. The faction said they could help with putting a special slide down from a hatch in the production line that he could use to leave the planet.

Being unable to take anything away with him in case he was spotted leaving he rushed to the production line. It was surprisingly difficult walking or doing anything with his magnification problems but he knew it was imperative. They were watching him he knew, so he must be extra vigilant.

He cautiously looked around to make sure no one was watching and then opened his escape route. Climbing on it he clung to the hatch with his feet so he could close it behind him. With a loud whoosh he was gone, no longer on planet Zig and he was safe, or would be when he reached the next planet.

....

At first all Zigzag saw was blackness. He was still going down the slide which seemed to go on for ever. Suddenly he was enveloped by a bright yellow light that blinded him at first. He couldn't work out what was happening. Was it a spaceship he had come across?

A voice came from deep inside, "So Zigzag I make you supervisor and then you try to leave."

Zigzag gasped! It was K! How did he know about the attempted escape so soon? Surely the Special Leaf can't have reported him yet, there hadn't been enough time, unless…. No, surely not, it couldn't be one of the faction against K. That was the only thing that made sense though. There was a traitor in their midst and now he had no way of warning the others or to finding how who it was.

"I am picking you up, and taking you back to face the ultimate punishment," said K in a tone which boded ill for Zigzag.

Zigzag tried to think quickly, there had to be a way of escaping. He couldn't let K take him back and make an example of him. He looked to the side trying to work out if he could jump. There was no guarantee if he would be safe though as it could lead to certain death, jumping into the unknown blackness beyond. The alternative was also not an option, he couldn't let K capture him and take him back.

He took a deep breath and did it, he leapt into the blackness, hoping to land somewhere quickly. He heard a roar from behind and realised K was following. The spaceship was closing in on him rapidly. What could he do?

Flapping his arms and legs he tried to weave from side to side as he hurtled further downwards at breathtaking speed. The roar of the spaceship was gaining on him. Ahead he caught the glimpse of light. Could it be safety? Was it another planet? He had so many questions, was there life on this new planet? Was he going to be safe or would he be in further danger? He had nothing to lose and everything to gain. Flapping arms and legs with all his might he tried guiding himself to the glow before him. The glare of light got brighter the closer he got.

....

Zig Zag was taken to the planet leader, Joffo. Apparently he had landed on the planet Jof.

Joffo smiled warmly at the newcomer. "Welcome to Jof. I see you are from Zig."

"Yes," replied Zigzag, pleased that things seemed to have worked out. There was something about Joffo that reassured him. He felt drawn to him.

"We have heard a lot of bad reports about Zig now K is leader."

"I had to make a rapid escape. They discovered myself and a few others were trying to overthrow K."

"Not good news. I hope you are not a trouble maker. We like peace here if you are staying."

"Sounds good to me," said Zigzag. "That's all I want. To live a peaceful life in safety."

"Well I will leave you for now. Loggo here, will show you around the planet and you can meet some of the folk that live here. Once again, welcome to Jof."

Joffo lifted his foot up and used it to make a salute. Zigzag was soon to learn this salute was a greeting between them all. He took a long time to get the hang of it as it was so different from what he was used to. He, like everyone on Zig, had very short stumpy legs.

Loggo was very pleasant and Zigzag felt as if he had made a friend already.

"Our planet thrives on this green food substance, which grows wild. We all help with picking it which is then shared out equally amongst us."

Zigzag felt he was going to really like living here. He was lucky, not many could say they had escaped from the evil K and the Special Leaf and lived to testify to what was happening. Living on such a peaceful planet was going to be blissful, after the constant fear he had left behind on Zig.

Someone rushed over and said, "Loggo who is this? He looks strange. Why is he walking on his hands?"

"This is Zigzag, from Zig. Zig this is Gloddo."

Gloddo saluted and poor Zig tried to return it but fell over in the attempt. Gloddo laughed and said, "You will get there with practice."

"I'm not sure about that," said Zigzag ruefully.

Loggo took him back to the main area where he had met Joffo. "This is where we gather to eat. Everyone will be here soon."

Zigzag felt a moment of anxiety, but was soon put at his ease when others started to arrive and spoke only with friendliness to him. They all saluted and laughed at his attempts to return it. They found him a strange species, but were nevertheless welcoming.

He had been there a couple of weeks when he was called to the main area to meet Joffo.

"How are you settling in?" asked Joffo, pleasantly.

"Everyone is nice. I am more relaxed than I have ever been."

"That is brilliant. I have had some communication from K asking if anyone had landed here from your planet….now don't look so worried, I didn't say anything about you. He believes no one has landed here. I have sent informants to take a look at what is going on there. Don't worry no one would have seen them. They are invisible when they leave this planet. They reported back to me earlier today and what I heard was not good."

Zigzag was very worried and couldn't keep it from Joffo.

"It seems a few members have been tortured and destroyed by K and his minions for allegedly trying to overthrow him as leader."

Zigzag paled at the news. There obviously had been a traitor in their midst. He told Joffo about it who nodded grimly.

Joffo said, "I have been in touch with our neighbouring planet Pod and we have decided some action needs to take place. We believe that if K is allowed to continue having more power then he may try to take over other planets.

Zigzag gasped at this news. He had never thought about it and neither had other members of the faction. "What can we do though?" he queried.

"We have decided that both our planets will join together and come up with some strategy to attack and destroy K. This is where you come in. We need information. How did you leave the planet for example. How do people land there?"

"I left through an escape hatch that is in the production line. I'm not sure it's possible for anyone to land there as there is a bubble that surrounds them. The slide from the escape hatch doesn't come here. I don't know where it goes."

"That gives us something to go on whilst we work out the details. Thank you. I will not require you to be involved as for you to go anywhere near them puts you at risk. I will of course keep you informed."

It was a few days later that Zigzag was informed the manoeuvre was to take place that day. He wasn't given any details in case it went wrong and K could work out where he was.

There was an extremely loud noise and the whole planet was lit with a dazzling bright light. Zigzag had to take his eyes off temporarily as it was too much for him. The noise he could just about tolerate.

It lasted sometime before everything settled down again. Zigzag went to the main area, sure it had been connected with Zig. He met Joffo, there who had a big grin on his face. He spoke saying, "We did it! K no longer exists, in fact the whole planet has been destroyed." Seeing the look of horror on Zigzag's face he continued, "We had no choice. When they realised what was happening, everyone formed a shield around the planet to protect K."

Zigzag was pleased it was all over but he mourned the planet's destruction but Joffo had made it clear he was welcome to make his life on Jof. He continued to live a nice peaceful life. He even managed to salute with practice.

Never Forget The Past

Samuel stood there amongst many others crowded around the wire. Like everyone else he was skeletal in appearance, bald headed. His stick like legs barely able to hold him up. They watched the lorries trundling up to the wire. They were finally going to be free of the nightmare. Samuel was fifteen but looked more like a ninety year old. He couldn't believe his eyes, couldn't believe it was all over and he would be released.

He turned to the person next to him to say, "It's over!" His voice was barely audible, due to extreme weakness from the starvation and dehydration they had been forced to endure under the Nazi regime. This was Burgen Belsen a notorious concentration camp that housed Jews, ill treated, starved and killed. Samuel was one of the lucky ones, many were not and had died.

The gates opened, but the inmates were too weak to cheer their rescuers.

Reg was one of the British troops to liberate the camp. He tried to hide the horror he felt as he went in, seeing these stick like figures and many piles more laying around dead. He couldn't move at first as he tried to take in the full horror of what he was seeing. He was seeing the worst example of mans inhumanity to man right before him. He tried hiding the tears that came to his eyes, thinking, "How could anyone do this? These poor people, what must they have endured?"

It was obvious that many of those still alive would not survive, they were too far gone.

Samuel tried to reach the lorry along with many others but found he could no longer stand, his legs gave way and he fell to the ground. Laying his head down it looked as if rescue had come too late for him.

"Hello can you hear me?" asked a voice in a language he didn't understand.

He tried opening his eyes, but even that was too much, all he managed was to blink.

"This one is barely alive," the voice called to another.

Men rushed over and looked down at Samuel with eyes full of tears. He felt himself being gently lifted and carried away but still unable to respond in any way.

It was days later before he opened his eyes and looked at the nurse smiling down at him. "You are back with us now," she said in German.

He looked around, disorientated. He seemed to be in a comfortable bed, not the hard boards he had been forced to lay on for years.

Seeing his confusion the nurse spoke again, "You are safe now. You are in hospital in Germany."

Samuel was horrified to discover he was in Germany.

"It's all right, it's over, you are safe now. No one will ever hurt you again."

It took many months for Samuel to recover, but very slowly he got his strength back. He started putting on weight again so that he looked more alive and human. Psychologically was a different matter altogether. He jumped and cowered in his bed at the slightest sound. He needed lights on all the time. Nightmares raged in him when he slept. He was completely alone in the world now, none of his family had survived what became known as the Holocaust.

Once stronger he became determined that the world must never forget what happened to him and millions of others. He spent the rest of his life talking to anyone who would listen to his story. One of such horror no one who heard him speak could ever ignore.

The End of the Tunnel

Jane was always being told there was light at the end of the tunnel, but it didn't feel like it. Recently divorced, now a single mum of two, a boy and girl aged 11 and 13. Abigail could be really difficult when she wanted to be, argumentative and a bully. Gary was the opposite, a quiet, studious boy. Jane really struggled to keep Abigail on the straight and narrow, but it was hard work. She had got into a bad crowd at school right after her father had walked out on them to go and live with another woman.

Jane had also been made redundant the previous year and still hadn't found a job.

Everything was now getting on top of her and she didn't know how much more she could take. Abigail had just been suspended from school again for bullying another girl just to add to the stress building up inside Jane. She wished she could go into a soundproofed room and just scream and scream a bit more.

Life was becoming difficult financially as well without a job to bring some money in. Living on state benefits just wasn't enough to live on. She had a job interview the next day but didn't want to get her hopes up. She couldn't bear another knock back.

Everything was just becoming too hard right now.

Before leaving for her job interview the next day she insisted that Abigail should spend the day concentrating on homework. She knew it wouldn't happen but trying to get through to her daughter was becoming imperative before she really went off the rails.

On arrival for her interview she was told to wait in an attractive room with comfortable chairs. She sat back in one, looking around the walls at all the certificates lining them. This was a highly prestigious law firm and she had applied for a secretarial job there.

She was shown into a light airy office, sunlight streaming through the windows. She turned her attention to the man sitting behind a desk. He smiled warmly at her and she felt herself blushing. He was a good looking thirty something with a mop of brown hair which fell almost across his left eye. Jane was instantly attracted to him although she was sure he must be married or at the very least attached. He didn't wear a wedding ring she noticed but that didn't mean anything these days. The interview went better than she hoped for and was offered the job straight away. She discovered she would be working with Paul, the name of the good looking guy. She was to start in a months time when her predecessor was to leave.

She went home, walking with a jaunty air. Surprised, she found   Abigail sitting at the table doing homework as requested. She even apologised to her mum. There was no explanation for why her behaviour had changed but Jane didn't care she was just overjoyed to see the difference.

Things finally seemed to be looking up. Maybe there was light at the end of the tunnel after all.

Jane had been in her new job for a couple of months and was loving it. She didn't find it particularly taxing though. It would have been nice to use her brain occasionally but she was just grateful to have a job. She found it increased her self esteem. The break up of her marriage no longer affected her as it had done previously. She was too busy to think about it. Besides she was finding herself attracted to her new boss. She stole glances frequently when she hoped he wasn't looking. He had a mop of hair that fell automatically over one eye which appealed greatly to her.

She occasionally went out with a few of her colleagues. Sometimes to the pub or a meal. Her life was looking up.

Both her children were doing well. Even Abigail who had been getting into a lot of trouble at school was settling down. She would never be a good girl but at least she would get down to doing her homework on time. She had stopped bullying others as well. Jane never knew what it was that had brought about this change but she was happy with it all the same.

Her thoughts these days were taken up with Paul, her boss. She knew he was single from the others in the office. She didn't know how to deal with him on a day to day basis because of the feelings she had for him. She saw no evidence that they were reciprocated. She just hoped she didn't blush when he spoke to her. None of the others had cottoned on to her attraction to Paul so she hoped she was getting away with it.

Unfortunately her feelings hadn't gone unnoticed by the office gossip Marjorie. So far, word hadn't reached the two people concerned, but it was becoming common knowledge amongst the rest of the staff. Sophie, Jane's friend at work did her best to keep it from her as she knew it would embarrass her if she were to find out. Jane was quiet and unassuming in personality and wasn't one to wear her emotions on her sleeve. Her general demeanour made it very strange for Marjorie or anyone else to pick up on Jane's attraction to Paul. Sophie still couldn't work out how anyone could suspect anything. Jane hadn't actually done anything to cause the gossip. It didn't take much for Marjorie and if there wasn't any she was quite likely to make something up and spread it around the office as if it were truth.

Paul wasn't as totally unaware of Jane as she thought. He was very aware of her. His feelings for her seemed to grow stronger with each passing day. He hadn't had a proper relationship with anyone before. Yes, he had gone out with women but it never worked out for long. He worried about asking her but was worried his feelings were not reciprocated. He knew she was separated from her husband and was worried about rushing things. He didn't want to push her away. It was only when the rumours reached his ears that he started to wonder if there was any truth in them. Could he really arouse something inside her? Somehow he had to find out, but he was unsure how to without her guessing what he was up to. He decided to mull it over for a few days, not wanting to frighten her off. She was a good employee, he couldn't risk losing her altogether.

A few days later Jane noticed Paul was glancing at her. She wondered if he was returning her feelings. At lunch when she was eating her sandwiches with Sophie she decided to broach the subject.

"Do you think Paul likes me?" she queried bluntly.

"Well that's not subtle," laughed Sophie. "I don't know, I haven't noticed anything but I'll pay more attention."

Sophie too, realised Paul seemed to be paying Jane more attention than was warranted. She started thinking of how she could help these two get together. It was clear they both felt the same but how to make them see it and take it further was the question.

Sophie decided to be honest with Jane and decided to drop subtle hints to Paul in the hope one of them would make the first move.

Paul couldn't believe what he was hearing when Sophie spoke to him bluntly. She made it clear they needed their heads knocking together as it was obvious they liked each other.

Paul decided to bite the bullet and ask Jane out. Totally stunned Jane accepted. They soon became a couple and so began their whirlwind romance. Of course Marjorie was glowing and boasting to everyone that she had seen it first.

Behind Closed Doors

Anne walked past number 13 and shook her head helplessly. Jean always seemed so cowed and browbeaten. Anne wished she could do something but she had no proof that there was even a problem. She had her suspicions though. She'd tried approaching Jean but she always avoided answering any questions. Anne had the impression that Jean was too scared to speak. It was a problem. Impossible to know what went on behind closed doors.

Anne had tried to find out what was going on. Jean wasn't going to speak to her quite obviously. She had tried speaking to other neighbours but met with a couldn't care less attitude. Long gone were the days where neighbours helped and looked out for each other. The police wouldn't intervene without evidence they had told her. In fact, she had the impression they saw her as just a nosy neighbour rather than a concerned citizen. She had kept her distance from Jean's husband, not wanting to cause more trouble for Jean.

Yesterday, she had caught a glimpse of Jean and her arms had been covered in bruises. There were two children to think of as well which worried Anne even more. The children were both early teens and appeared vulnerable by their appearance not that she had seen much of them. What was happening to them and what were they witnessing? She had never noticed bruising on the children and she had done her best to have a look – surreptitiously of course. It concerned her that the children were witnessing the alleged abuse. The psychological effects didn't bear thinking about. Today, the curtains were closed. So there was no way she could look to see what might be happening. She had worked out that it was a bad sign when they were closed. What was she supposed to do? The police wouldn't be interested in this when she couldn't even say there was a problem.

She went indoors and sat down, worn out from her shopping trip. She closed her eyes for a minute and dozed off. She was jolted awake by a scream. Was that coming from number 13? If there had been an incident, she couldn't avoid taking action now. A scream surely meant something was very wrong.

She went out and warily knocked on the door. When no one responded she called through the letter box asking if everything was all right. There was still no answer although she thought she heard the faintest sound. She called again, saying she would call the police if no one answered.

"Get lost," called a voice. Not a masculine voice as she had expected, but the voice of a child, probably female.

"Please let me in to speak to your mum," she called again.

"I won't tell you again. If you don't leave us alone you will be sorry you nosy bitch."

What did that mean? Why would a child be making threats like that?   Maybe they were just frightened and were probably just trying to protect themselves and their mum. Anne wasn't prepared to leave things as they were so she began to return to her house where she intended to call the police. She was a bit confused, expecting a man to answer.

When the police arrived they tried to gain access. This time the door was opened and revealed the true horror of what had been happening. Jean and her husband Tom were laying on the floor hands and legs bound tightly together. Standing over them was a boy and a girl who looked to be in their early teens. They were each holding knives which were pointed at their parents.

When Anne realised what this all meant she was shocked. For whatever reason it seemed as if the children were the abusers not Tom. The children obviously needed help. It made Anne question what had happened to make the children act with such violence towards their parents. At least now this mess would be sorted out and Jean and Tom would be able to live safely in future.

Surrounded

Sandra looked around her, everything seemed the same but felt different. She couldn't explain it. She looked across at the television and sure enough it happened again. The telly was talking to her. Was this normal? She couldn't work it out. She listened intently and became frightened, she was in danger. She stood up and looked all around her. Where was the danger coming from? The walls began closing in on her, she had to escape, but where to.

She felt as if someone was behind her trying to strangle her. Her throat was closing up and she was struggling to breathe. Panic set in. She tried forcing the hands away from her neck but they only squeezed harder. It was time to get out, run away. She felt so disorientated. Where was the door? She found it just before blackness closed in on her, before the strangulation completed it's job. She rushed out and breathed some deep relaxing breaths. Fresh air, she could breathe again. The person had gone.

Quickly walking away, needing to run but at the same time not wanting to draw attention to herself. She couldn't work out why everyone was staring at her as she passed. She thought they were waiting to attack her and increased her pace to a steady trot.

Sandra had forgotten she needed shoes and had rushed out in her slippers without even noticing the freezing cold around her. She only had a thin top on having not thought she needed a coat.

She had no idea where she was going, she had no money with her. She thought about ringing her dad but decided against it. She couldn't take that risk. She didn't know who to trust. For all she knew they may have got to him and turned him against her.

She didn't know where to go for safety. Everything seemed to be speaking to her, voices coming from all directions. She turned in circles trying to work out which way led to safety. She collapsed, putting her head in her hands.

"It's all right. You are safe now. We'll look after you," said the reassuring voice of a nurse.

The station

She looked around her. Everything seemed strange. People rushing here and there. No time to stop and help as they rushed in all directions looking down at their feet. There was a lot of jostling in the crowds. It was always like this though. It was a busy station. Everyone rushing on and off trains in a hurry to get where they were going.

She tried approaching someone and tentatively enquired, "Have you seen a girl of about twelve? She is wearing a blue flowery top and jeans."

The stranger didn't even bother to answer, just carried on her way.

What was she to do? She needed to find her quickly before anything dreadful happened to her. Her mouth was dry and sweat was dripping down her face. She knew she must smell from the sweat, although she had used deodorant that morning.

Where was Josephine? She should be there by now waiting to be picked up. She tried calling her name over and over, more desperate with each cry.

"Excuse me, you seem distressed, can I help at all?" asked a kindly voice to her left.

"Oh please, I was supposed to meet my young daughter here but I can't find her. She's twelve years old and was visiting my parents for the weekend."

"It's so busy she is probably looking for you as well. You may have missed her in the crowds. Why don't you come with me and we can get her name called over the tannoy," said the gentleman.

She turned and looked at him with interest. He was a tall, grey haired man with a beard and moustache. There was a twinkle in his brown eyes which told of a strong sense of humour. There was a gentleness about his features which drew her to him.

"Thank you, that would be really kind of you."

He looked more closely at her, seeing the distraught look on her face. Frown lines told of her worry. "I'm sure you'll find each other soon," he said trying to reassure her.

They walked together to the customer services desk. Seeing that the woman beside him was too distressed and lost for words he spoke for her. Very quickly a call was put out for Josephine.

They waited together, he reluctant to leave someone who looked so hopeless, despairing. No one came forward despite the call being put out twice.

Suddenly someone rushed forward and said, "Ann, here you are! I've been looking all over the station for you. Come on let's get you home."

She looked up at her husband with a vague, empty look in her eyes and nodded.

Her husband turned to the the man who looked confused and said, "Sorry to have bothered you. Josephine is the name of our baby who was stillborn twelve years ago. My wife still looks for her every year. It was at this station she went into labour."

The Voice

Sally walked hurriedly past the mirror, not risking even a sideways glance. She knew if she did, the figure living there would start talking to her again. She couldn't bear to see that face. The penetrating stare was too much, as if it could read into her very soul. This used to be a common occurrence until she worked out how to avoid it. It didn't mean she was permanently free though because she wasn't. The figure sometimes came out to torment her.

Sally was a tall girl in her mid twenties. She had silky jet black hair which she kept tied up in a ponytail. People told her she should wear it loose so it would float naturally about her face. Emma, her colleague, had only told her this yesterday, commenting what a beauty she would be if she only tried it. Sally knew differently though. There would never be anything beautiful about her.

Sally was very thin, anorexic some might say, but she knew otherwise. The voice in the mirror was always tormenting her.

"You are too fat just a blob. Stop eating then you'll get thin. No one will want to know you. You're the ugliest person in the world," and so it would go on.

Sally had just finished her regular gym class when the taunting began again. Sally stood there against the wall, breathless from the exercise. The more the voice spoke telling her how worthless she was the more hunched up her shoulders became and her head bowed low. Occasionally she looked in the direction of the voice that she was listening to intently.

"You are worthless, no one wants to know you. Don't even bother speaking to anyone they will ignore you."

Emma, also in the gym class, came up to Sally breathless and panting, "That was a good work out today don't you think?" she queried. Receiving no answer she glanced at Sally saying, "You all right love? You seem distracted."

"What, oh yeah, what did you say?" Sally reddened as she realised she had no idea what Emma had been talking about, so in tune with the voice as she was.

"I said it was a good workout today," repeated Emma.

"Yeah I suppose so," replied Sally abruptly, not really wanting to get into conversation.

The voice had been telling her she was not to speak to others as she was not worthy. Everyone knew what she was really like and didn't want to know her.

Sally glanced across the room to where a group of women stood gossiping together.

"You see those women over there, they are talking about you. They are saying how gross you look and how could someone like you bother with gym. It's pointless." Sally could believe that as she was certain they kept stealing glances in her direction and laughing about her. She looked at Emma who was still standing with her silently. She really appreciated the older woman's support. She longed to reach out to this lady who had showed her nothing but kindness in and outside of work. Something always stopped her. That niggling doubt that the voice always planted in her mind that no one would want to know given a choice.

The group of women left without so much as a backward glance at Sally. It was just the two of them left now.

Emma reached out to touch Sally's arm, but she immediately jerked away. Emma let her arm drop feeling slightly foolish. She didn't know what was wrong but Sally always repudiated all attempts of friendship but Emma wasn't one to give up easily.

"Why don't we go and get a coffee," suggested Emma. She was trying to draw Sally away from what was clearly frightening her for a look of abject terror had crossed her face briefly before being replaced by blankness.

Sally surprised herself and Emma by giving a slight nod although she stayed silent. Emma having learnt her lesson didn't take Sally's arm again just saying, "Come on then. There's a coffee shop in the next street that is spectacular. A bit on the expensive side, but worth every penny."

Sally nodded and followed her new friend outside. Her hope was the voice would not interfere so she might be able to make a true friendship for once.

Pop

Pop stepped out of the spaceship and looked around. His ears poked up and eyes popped out. He noticed everything in his field of vision was a mass of green. Was the whole planet green or just this area? Were there any living beings on this planet? Pop had been sent to investigate with the possibility of seeing if Poppians could settle there.

Pop moved away cautiously. All his antennae raised, alert to the possibility of danger. If he looked above him he saw a vast expanse of blue interspersed with white fluff like cotton wool. Also, a bright yellow light shone down dazzling him with its brightness. At first glance, he wasn't sure if it would be possible to set up home here, wherever here was. He was used to relative darkness on Popple.

He had lots of questions forming in his mind that he needed answers to. That was if he could investigate this planet further. He needed to shield his eyes so he put them back in their sockets. This only gave him small relief from this radiant light shining down on him.

He began walking straight ahead to see what he would come across. He had an innate curiosity that was part of his race. So far they inhabited three planets and were looking into taking over another.

He heard noises coming from somewhere. He continued on wondering what the sound was. He started to think the planet might be populated by some alien race. He warily went in the direction the noise was coming from. Soon he came across some living beings rapidly moving around. They seemed to know exactly where they were going as they were rushing around purposefully.

He drew closer, deciding he would have to try to interact if he were going to find out anything. The green he had landed in had disappeared to grey with white lines going along it. These beings were stopped at the edge looking both ways before crossing the grey. He approached slowly and carefully, not wanting to frighten anyone and not wanting to prompt any aggression from these alien beings.

"He…hello," he stammered, approaching what looked like a miniature being.

The being turned to him, shock and something akin to fear showing on his face. He tried hurrying away but Pop held his hand out holding him back. "Please talk to me, I need to know where I am and a bit about this planet. I've just landed here."

The being smiled shyly. "You are on planet earth," he said. "Where are you from?" he queried politely, although not sure he wanted to get into conversation with this queer stranger.

"I'm from Popple and I was sent here to investigate the planet and decide if we could populate the area. Why had the land changed from green to grey?"

"You are in the town. Back in the direction you have come from is countryside which is a lot of green fields and hedgerows. We are called human beings as we live here. If we carry on a long this road you will come across buildings as it is a residential area.

That means people live there," said Dan, explaining as he saw the puzzled look on Pop's face.

They continued in silence neither knowing what to say. It was a few minutes later they reached what Pop saw as tall, red brick buildings. "What are these?" he queried.

"Buildings. It is where we live and some of these buildings are offices so we work there," he replied, moving his arm in a wide arc to indicate a large area.

"It's time for offices to shut so we're all going home for the day," said Pop's new friend. "You can come home with me if you like," said the human. Pop had learnt occupants of this planet were known as humans.

They went to the home of this strange being called human. Pop was curious and looked around at everything. There were things with wheels on that travelled along the grey ground. What was it the human had called them? Roads which those strange things called cars travelled along.

It wasn't long before they arrived home and they went in.

"I'll just put the heating on as it is quite cold," said the human.

"Do you have a name?"

"Yes, I'm Dan. This is where I live with another human. She isn't home yet but should be soon."

"Just one human? I don't understand," said Pop who was used to living in one large area with all other inhabitants of the planet.

Seeing the puzzlement on Pop's face, Dan said, "You saw all the buildings we passed on the way home, well those are where other humans live. We live separately or in family groups, meaning we live with people related to us by birth or marriage."

Pop looked even more confused at this.

Later he discovered it seemed to be getting dark. Dan got up and pressed something which caused the room to light up. Again Pop was dazzled by the brightness that filled the room. Dan on seeing this, explained the need for light to see what they were doing. Pop in turn, explained that his planet was always dark. No brightness was there. He was starting to believe that this strange planet would be unsuitable for the needs of the Poppians. He decided he would go back tomorrow and report his findings to the governor and hope that it would be the end of it.

The Room

The room was almost bare except for a bed and a couple of chairs. The table in the corner contained a wash jug, ready for use in the morning when Ed woke up, that is assuming he even slept at all. He didn't dare get out of bed and creep across the floor to go to his parents room. His footsteps on the bare floor echoed around the room and could be heard throughout his grandparents cottage.

He couldn't say what it was about the room, there was just something. His parents were always telling him there was nothing, but they didn't understand, they didn't hear the whispers that he heard throughout the night.

The whole room had an eerie quality to it, even the pictures on the walls seemed to come alive. They lit up when the stars and moon shone through the tiny window making the people in them become vivid and real.

It didn't matter what time of year, the room was always freezing to Ed. He dreaded hearing his parents telling him they were going to his grandparents for a week. He didn't want anyone to misunderstand him, he loved his grandparents very much but the house was another thing altogether. It was that room. The damp, musty smell would fill his lungs as he inhaled. There was no heating in the room only an empty fireplace which made it even more creepy. The windows creaked, rattled and banged making him jump. To Ed it added to the sinister atmosphere of the room. He had read in books that ghosts liked cold places and inhabited old buildings. This was certainly one of those. They didn't even have an indoor toilet.

Every night he would check under the bed to make sure there was no one hiding there waiting to pounce as soon as he fell asleep. Sometimes his mum would sit in one of the rickety old chairs until then, but he always worried the chair would collapse under her. It always wobbled from the uneven floor or the legs not being of equal length, he wasn't sure which.

He would curl up under his red covered duvet which he insisted taking with him. It brought the room alive and gave it a warmth through the vibrancy of the colour, better than the austere grey walls. Some nights when he was particularly cold and frightened he would curl himself into a foetal position. Covering himself completely so he couldn't be seen by any presence there might be in the room.

"Whoosh! Whoosh!" came the sound, startling him awake. He hadn't even been aware he had dozed off. He didn't dare move or make a sound, even holding his breath so nothing would alert the presence that he was there. Not even calling his parents he lay stiff to all appearances dead. He never knew where the sound came from but he assumed it was under his bed as there was nowhere else it could hide. Concealed it had to be, as it was only ever a sound. There was nothing to be seen, no shape, no shadow anywhere.

The cock a doodle doo of the cockerel every morning brought reassurance to Ed. It meant he would soon be able to get out of bed and leave the room.

Looking out of the window to the green and yellow fields beyond the small path that led to the outdoor toilet was always a pleasure. The peace and tranquillity always soothed his anxious, overactive mind. Soon he would be back home again in his lovely warm modern house with no ghosts or monsters to haunt him.

The Mud

Squelch!! Squelch!! Plip Plop tried moving along the ground but was finding it increasingly hard going. A mud like substance was overtaking the planet. Plip Plop was responsible for collecting some for analysis, passing it to the super scientists who would try and find a way of clearing it up and preventing it from returning. Plip Plop didn't think they had time though as it was getting deeper with every minute that went by.

He was about to go and report to the Eye that things were getting worse, when a very large ball of muddy stuff fell on top of him. For a moment he panicked, thinking he was being buried alive. He couldn't shake himself free so he would just have to go to Eye as he was.

The Eye spoke as soon as Plip Plop appeared before it. "That doesn't look good," he said.

"It is horrible out there and building up over time," responded Plip Plop. "Is it all right if I make a suggestion Eye?" he queried tentatively, as it was not usually allowed to give advice to the Eye or disagree. The punishment could be death.

"Speak servant Plip Plop," commanded the Eye.

"I think you should consider evacuating the planet," he said timidly.

The Eye appeared to give this some thought before replying, "You really think this is the best solution?"

"I do oh blessed one," said Plip Plop, bowing low in deference to the Eye's position as leader.

"I don't want to unless absolutely necessary. We haven't looked at other planets to see which one would suit our needs and be a viable option for the sustenance of our people."

"I understand what you say, but we are not going to survive here much longer. We don't know where this is coming from or if there is anything we can do to stop it."

The Eye nodded in understanding and Plip Plop continued, "I did have a thought that this might be coming from somewhere else wanting to invade and take over this planet."

"Hmm, you have a good point but we can't leave if that is the case we must stay and fight back. This is war. Do all you can to establish what is happening here by trying to determine what this is and getting rid of it," instructed the Eye.

Plip Plop bowed low before leaving the presence of the Eye.

He rushed to the laboratory needing to get back to work as quickly as possible. He looked at the dark brown, glutinous substance under the microscope. He peered at charts containing information from other planets to try and determine where it was from. His eyes started to glaze over as he stared at them. Suddenly he shouted, he thought he had discovered what was happening. Getting up he rushed back to the Eye.

"I've found it! I've found it!" he exclaimed, forgetting to bow.

"Ahem," said the Eye trying to draw his attention to his serious error before it was too late.

Plip Plop was far too excited to notice his oversight and continued speaking, "It came from planet earth, they call it mud. It had been caused by too much wet stuff coming down in torrents. It has then drained from there and come to us. We have never had any trouble from the earthlings before so I think it is an accident that they are unaware of."

"I tend to agree with you. We need to try and suction it off and hope no more rains down on us. Meanwhile I need to decide on your punishment for not bowing before me. Under section 5 I hereby sentence you, Plip Plop, to death by full immersion in this mud."

The Eye was very pleased with himself, he had suspected Plip Plop's attitude for some time. He had arranged with planet earth to fill the planet with mud as the best method of killing off anyone who dared question his authority.

Lost

Adam looked around him, everything was dark and he had no idea where he was. His car had broken down on the side of the road. He tried calling for help but his mobile had no signal so he walked along the road for a bit before venturing into the woods.

It had been okay earlier when it was still daylight. He had hoped the detour would enable him to make a short cut to the next town but it wasn't turning out like that. He admitted to himself that he was hopelessly lost. For all he knew he was going around and round in circles. He decided to mark the trees so he would know if he was coming back to the same point.

Hearing a noise, he stood still to see if he could work out what it was or where it was coming from. There it was again. It sounded like a whimper nearby.

"Hello, is anyone there," he called quietly, not wanting to frighten anyone, for by now he was sure it was a human noise.

"Wh…who is it?" asked the voice quietly.

"My name is Adam. Who are you?"

"Estelle."

"Hello Estelle, I'm totally lost. Do you know where we are? I'm on my way to Ravensfield but my car broke down. I thought walking through the woods would get me home quicker."

"We're in the woods near the town you speak of."

Something about the tone of her voice and the wording made shivers go down his spine. Something wasn't quite right, but he couldn't put his finger on it.

"Could you come out from wherever you are and point me in the direction I need to go?" he asked politely.

From behind a tree which was surrounded by thick foliage this person stepped out. He was surprised to see a diminutive figure before him, which despite her height was definitely a female adult.

He held out his hand which she took in a firm grip. So firm he had to avoid yelling in protest. There was something sharp digging in the palm of his hand. He assumed it must be long nails.

"I'll take you to the edge of the woods and point you in the right direction."

"Thank you that would be so kind of you."

They walked in silence for a while, before Adam said, "So Estelle where are you from? It seems unusual for someone to be out in the woods at this late hour."

"I know these woods like the back of my hand," she said, without offering any sort of explanation.

He accepted this, but again felt that same feeling of uneasiness.

"We turn left here."

In front of Adam he could just about make out a small hut. Something was definitely not right, but he didn't know how to get away.

Estelle slowed down, indicating the hut in front of her. "Go inside," she said in a no nonsense commanding tone in her voice.

He stood still not wanting to obey her.

"Go in now," she said again, giving him no option of refusal.

He looked at her helplessly. He was in deep trouble, that much he knew. He took a few steps towards the hut closely followed by Estelle who put a firm hand on his back, guiding him in the direction she wanted him to go.

At the hut he opened the door and went inside. He looked around him. A shaft of light shone enough for Adam to see his surroundings. The hut was very tiny and bare except for a table and two chairs.

"Sit," commanded Estelle.

"Who are you? What do you want with me?"

"I have been sent to conduct an experiment on humans to see if you could live on our planet."

He was quiet for a few minutes, trying to take in what she had just said. It didn't make sense. Was she delusional?

"Can you explain?" he asked.

"I have just told you. I am unable to engage in anymore talk of where I am from."

"How did you know I was going to come through the woods?"

"I set a trap up along the road to catch unsuspecting motorists then I watched and waited."

"What happens now?"

"We wait for my vehicle to pick us up and take us to our next destination."

He looked at her and noticed she was changing. She no longer looked an innocent woman but looked like a strange creature which was slowly turning brown before his very eyes. Her hair disappeared as did her nose. Her hands became webbed like ducks.

A strange noise could be heard in the distance which got louder as it drew closer.

It stopped. Someone walked into the hut and spoke to the creature. "I see you got us a fine specimen of a human for us this time Edell."

"That's what I thought," replied Edell, for that was her real name on her planet.

Steering Adam to the spaceship, he reluctantly climbed aboard. Everything was bright inside with lots of buttons and levers. This would have been interesting at any other time but all he knew was fear. Of course he had heard people talk about alien abduction but never in his wildest dreams had he thought it a real possibility, until now when it was happening to him.

The Holiday

They boarded the plane, highly excited, this was their first ever trip to America and they were really looking forward to it. They had booked a two weeks holiday in Florida at Disneyworld. It wasn't just that. They were going to meet Christine's mum for the first time. She had been adopted as a baby. She had always known she was adopted but it was only when her parents died in a car accident last year that she had decided to trace her biological parents. Her father was unknown but she had been in regular contact with her birth mother for the last six months.

The family of four were seated and ready to be off. Just behind them were a couple, one of whom looked vaguely familiar to Christine. Busy settling her two children down she paid little attention to them.

Soon they were underway but already the children were restless and bored.

"How much longer," whined David.

"It will be a few hours yet darling," said Christine, feeling already that this was going to be a very long flight.

Simon looked at her over the children's head and raised his eyebrows and pulled a face.

"Come on you two we talked about this remember. Let's play I spy."

"Dad we're not babies," complained Sharon.

"Don't act like one then."

"Excuse me, I couldn't help overhearing and I still like playing that game and I'm getting old now," said the gentleman in the seat behind them.

Christine turned round to smile gratefully at the man for his timely intervention. The smile froze on her face as she saw who was behind. It was Bernard. She hadn't thought of him in years and had no wish to think of him again.

"Christine it's really you! I can't believe it!" he exclaimed.

Simon looked questioningly at his wife. She didn't look happy at all. She had tensed up whereas just now she was relaxed and trying to occupy the kids.

"Bernard," she said abruptly.

"How many years has it been?" asked Bernard, seemingly oblivious to the tension that had sprung up.

"Not long enough," muttered Christine under her breath, so only Simon heard.

Something was very wrong here but he didn't know what. He had never seen his wife behave like this. She was usually so open and friendly towards everyone. He thought he knew everything about her but it seemed she had kept something of significance to herself. The had agreed no secrets when they got engaged but it seemed she hadn't kept her side of the bargain.

"I think you'd better tell me what this is about," said Simon.

"It's nothing," said Christine, turning her head away so Simon wouldn't see the tears. She had spent her entire adult life trying to forget Bernard and what had happened that night.

"Nothing! What do you mean? We had something special between us," said Bernard.

"Something special! Is that what you call it," she exploded. "I thought we were supposed to be going to the cinema together. Instead you said you had something to show me and you drove to that isolated spot…" she stopped suddenly, unable to go on as the tears came.

Simon leaned over and put his hand on her arm. "What is it darling? What happened?"

She shook her head.

"Daddy what's wrong with mummy?" asked Sharon.

"I don't know honey," he replied.

Turning back to his wife he saw extreme distress on her face. Imagining all sorts he turned to Bernard who shrugged.

"What did you do to her?"

"I didn't do anything she didn't want to do, honest," Bernard opened his hands palms up.

"What do you mean, nothing I didn't want?" screamed Christine.

"Shh," said Bernard. "We don't want the whole plane hearing our business."

"You mean you don't want everyone to know how you lured me to that place and tied me up before raping me."

There were gasps from others nearby who had heard every word of the exchange.

Simon stood up wanting to punch the man who had hurt his wife so badly.

"You agreed."

"You held a knife to my throat, what did you expect."

Simon pulled Bernard to his feet forming his hands into fists. An air steward came over and gave them both a warning. Simon sat back down. "This isn't over," he said.

"Leave it," said Christine, "He isn't worth it."

The rest of the flight took place in a tense silence which even the children picked up on and kept quiet.

Bleeding Heart

Chris looked up as his mum entered the room. "Are you all packed?" she asked.

He didn't respond because of the lump in his throat. His mum sat on the bed and tried to take his hand but he pulled away.

"Come on love, you know we have to make this move. It's best for your dad's job and we need to move closer to your grandparents. They're getting older and need more help."

Chris turned away, not wanting his mum to see the tears that he could no longer hold back. He wasn't quick enough however.

"I know you'll miss Lucy but there'll be other girls. You're too young to be so serious about one girl."

"How can you say that? We're sixteen. We love each other."

"You think you do, but when you meet others you will go out with them and meet someone who is special to you."

"You don't get it," he almost shouted. "We want to be together. We're going to get engaged when we're eighteen."

His mum shook her head and left the room. She felt for him, she really did, but knew that he would meet someone else. Both she and John, her husband hoped so. It wasn't that they didn't like Lucy, they did, but they both felt the couple were getting too serious.

On his own, Chris reached for his phone and checked messages. Yes, as expected there was one from the love of his life. He smiled as he read it.

"Love you."

He responded. They sent these texts all the time when they were not together. He phoned her, needing to hear her voice.

She answered straightaway.

"Hiya babe," he said smiling.

"Hello," she said in what she called her posh voice.

"Is your mum there?" he asked. She always put on that voice in front of her mum.

"Of course I can make tomorrow evening…history project…yes, we should get it finished if we spend all evening on it."

"See you tomorrow, love you babe."

He put the phone down. They went through the same code every time Lucy's mum was in listening distance. Her mum didn't approve of the two being together, but then she didn't think Lucy should have a boyfriend. She wrapped her precious daughter up in cotton wool, mollycoddling her. Lucy complained more than once that she felt suffocated.

He sighed, they only had a couple of days left before they moved to the other end of the country.

………

The day came for moving. He sent numerous texts to the love of his life. They promised to keep in touch by text and calls. They were determined to make this long distance relationship thing work. His mum was convinced he would meet someone else, but she didn't understand.

Over time he noticed that the texts he was receiving from Lucy were not as frequent and she didn't always respond to his. Eventually the texts and calls dwindled out completely.

House of Secrets

Clare and Dale got out of the car and stared with dismay at the house they had just inherited. It was very dilapidated, looking as if there had been no work done in years. There were cracks in the wall and the garden was overgrown to the point Clare could imagine all sorts of wildlife must have made it their home. With cracked and broken windows it was obvious a lot of work was needed.

They looked at each other and shrugged. Dale said, "Are you ready? I hate to think what the inside must look like."

"I was thinking the same thing. It looks dismal from here. I don't know why the old boy would even leave me this house. It's not as if I knew him."

"I know, but since he has we might as well look. Unfortunately, if we want to sell we will have to do extensive work on the place."

Clare taking Dale's arm led the way. She discovered she didn't even need the key as the door was not completely shut, being half off its hinges. They stepped inside and looked around with their heart sinking even lower at the sight that met them. It must have once been a nice kitchen but this was anything but nice. The wooden table was missing a leg and it was obvious very quickly that one of the remaining ones was a bit shorter than the others. Quickly leaving the room they entered what must have been a living room. There were just two chairs which didn't look very comfortable, being very upright and hard. The fireplace looked inviting. Clare could just imagine sitting by the fire on a cold winters night with a fire blazing in the grate. It would be nice and cosy. Dale looked at her, noticing the slight smile on her face and knew what she was thinking.

"That's right up your street that fireplace isn't it?"

"Oh yes, it definitely is. I love it! I can imagine sitting there of an evening and listening to the crackle of the flames with nothing but the fire to keep us warm," responded Clare. A bit more enthusiastic than she had previously been..

They thought of it as a mystery house because no one even knew about it or about this relative who had lived in it before his recent death. All that was known was that he was a bit of a recluse, an odd ball as her mother had referred to him, living there until he died.

"I don't know why he never spent money on this place. It could have been done up all nice. Keeping its period features would have added to its attraction," she said.

Clare wandered over to the mantelpiece and said, "Hey look at this! It's an old fashioned wireless set. It looks as if it belongs to the 1940s. There's no television. I wonder what he did all day without any entertainment other than the wireless."

"Would the wireless even work now?"

"Only one way to find out," she said attempting to switch it on. All her efforts were in vain, the knobs were stiff and seemed stuck. Shaking her head, she gave up trying.

"Never mind," said Dale putting his arm across his wife's shoulder.

She looked at him despondently, leaning into his comfortable frame. How nice it was to have her wonderful husband to bring warmth into this cold, dismal house.

They looked through the rest of the house seeing the same awful state of repair as they first encountered. It was depressing and made them shiver even though it was a very warm summers day in the outskirts of London. The paint was pealing from the walls and in places was brown with age. They discovered mould across the windows and in one corner of a window there was even moss growing. The floor was uneven which meant they were always watching their feet to avoid any accidents. Clare shivered, she hated all of this, being someone so orderly who hated mess of any sort. Seeing it set her teeth on edge.

"Well," said Dale when they were back outside. "That certainly needs a lot of work. I can't even get my head around it."

"I suppose we'll have to come back again and really take stock of the situation, making notes of what needs doing. I just can't imagine he was living in such conditions, it's inhumane," said Clare angrily.

"I suppose that is what he wanted. We have to respect his wishes.   Anyway he isn't here now so we have work to sort out to make it habitable. I think we should come back next weekend and see what's what. We'll know what to expect so will be able to take our time looking in detail."

"You know, I'm not even sure it can be done up. It looks as if it would be better off demolished, it needs so much work." Clare sighed, overwhelmed by it all.

. . . .

The following weekend they returned armed with notebooks and pens to make a start on noting what needed doing. They decided there was no need to do anything about the furniture that could just be thrown out, but the house was a different matter altogether.

At lunchtime they both gave a sigh of relief and stopped their lengthy note taking. They had decided to split up and Clare did the first floor while Dale did the ground floor.

They sat on the concrete and laid out their picnic lunch. Gratefully they sat on the rug Dale had the sense to take with them. Eating in companionable silence for a few minutes before Clare broke it to say, "This is going to take forever to go through. I have only done about half. I curse the day I answered the phone to the solicitor. If only I had not taken it we wouldn't be here now. We'd be getting on with our lives in blissful ignorance."

"Never mind, we will soon be finished and then we can leave it to the workman to get it up to scratch," said Dale comfortingly.

"I suppose so," said Clare, unenthusiastically.

"Look at it this way, we'll get a sense of achievement when we see the finished version. It's just another project to get our teeth into."

"I know you are right but I still feel overwhelmed by all the work needed."

They compared lists which were quite long and still more to go. Reluctantly they agreed to get back to work. They didn't want to have to come back at a later date to finish. Clare breathed a sigh of relief, it had been a long day and she just wanted to get back to civilised living conditions.

Dale put his arm around his wife and said, "At least we have finished this. Tomorrow we should look over the lists and see what needs to be done so that Monday I can start ringing around to get quotes. It won't be cheap."

Clare nodded in agreement, for she was so tired.

…………..

It was one day a few weeks later that Clare received a phone call from the contractors doing the work to say they had discovered something under the floor they had just dug up. It was agreed they would go and see what it was before deciding what to do with it.

A week later when both Clare and Dale had managed to get the day off work they set off to see what had been found. Surely it couldn't be too much.

On arrival one of the workers went out to meet them. "It seems to be some sort of notebook or diary that was kept."

Clare took it from him with grateful thanks. They stayed in the car to flip through the book together. It definitely seemed to be some sort of diary, the pages yellow with age.

"I can't understand why it was under the floor," said Clare. "Why would someone bury it?"

"Let's have a look to see what it's about. It must be of some importance to be hidden like that. We had better be careful as it looks quite fragile."

Wanting to have a quick look, they skimmed through. It seemed nothing of anything worth noting so they decided to go for a walk before beginning the journey back. They didn't inspect the house to see how the workmen were getting on.

When they got back home they sat down to take a longer look at the diary. One thing that leapt out at Dale was the age of it. "Hey this is interesting look how ancient this is. The first entry is earlier than the seventeenth century."

Clare looked over his shoulder to see what he was talking about. Clare with mounting interest wanted to read it through more thoroughly. She was a history enthusiast. Dale, knowing he had captured Clare's attention passed the book for her to read at her leisure.

"Hey, look here, this diary is mentioning executions at the Tower of London. This is like a thriller. I have to read more."

"What about executions at the Tower?"

"It just comments on one having taken place."

Clare had Dale's attention now. He could feel something stirring inside. To read something so many centuries old. It was a part of history linked to them. It was unbelievable that some ancestor in the past had written about the dark times in British history. Clare started reading extracts out loud so Dale would know what it said.

"August 10, 1612. Another failed attempt. Execution taken place."

"What does that mean?" queried Dale.

Clare shrugged. "I don't know, that's all it says. There are lots of entries like that one. It makes no reference as to what failed."

"How frustrating," replied Dale, who was now just as involved as Clare.

"Hey, wait a minute! I think I've found something," she exclaimed.

"What? What?" asked Dale almost snatching the book from his wife's hands.

"I don't believe it. Listen to this: *September 13, 1615, success at last! Execution couldn't take place. Prisoner disappeared without trace.*"

Clare and Dale looked at each other. They were totally captivated now. "How could a prisoner just disappear from there. It's impossible to disappear from a prison cell, unless he had help. Did one of the guards let him out?"

Clare shrugged. "It doesn't say. I just read the full entry."

"I didn't know anyone ever escaped before. I wonder if there is any way of finding out what was happening at the time. This whole diary seems to go in the same vein. This writer is fascinated by the Tower of London and executions. I suppose it is a bit macabre really, but I'm finding it rather thrilling."

Dale pulled his laptop towards them. He switched it on. He went straight to google to see what he could find about the Tower and its history in relation to the executions taking place there. He scrolled down, unable to find anything about escaped prisoners or searches being made. He read quickly just skimming the articles but nothing. "I can't find anything about escapees at all. If it even happened it must have been covered up well."

"It must have happened or why would someone bother to write a note about it in a diary. What I find strange is how the writer even knew about any escapes. If we can't find anything on the internet it obviously wasn't broadcast at the time," Clare said.

"It's a mystery all right," said Dale. "It's one I want to solve."

"Unfortunately we might never know. It all depends on what else is in the diary. I'm going back to the beginning and read it more thoroughly this time so we don't miss anything."

Dale nodded in agreement.

They did just that, reading well into the night. It was slow going as the handwriting was not always clear and also the sheer age of the diary and the yellowed pages didn't make it easier. They were having to guess at some of the words. Eventually Dale called it a day and suggested they should go to sleep and continue the following evening after work.

"It's Saturday tomorrow, silly."

They both laughed at Dale's mistake.

The next morning after breakfast they began again, unable to wait any longer.

"Hey I think I've found it! I can't believe it! It seems there was a secret network of people trying to rescue prisoners from the Tower to avoid execution."

"Let me see," demanded Dale eagerly.

"It talks of a secret passage leading into the Tower which they used to get in the condemned man's cells."

"Where was the secret passageway?" asked Dale although suspicion was already forming in his mind.

Clare jumped up and down excitedly.

"Calm down and tell me what it is."

"The secret passage is in that house. We dismissed it as a heap of junk but instead it's vitally important. Who would ever have guessed."

They were both excited at their discovery. Dale said, "Why don't we get ready and go now to see if we can find it?"

"We don't have a clue where it is though. We could spend a whole day and still not find it."

"Does it give any indication where we need to look?" asked Dale refusing to be put off.

Clare skimmed quickly trying to find more information. Like Dale she was thoroughly into this mystery and wanted to find it.

At last she broke the silence and almost shouted, "Here it is, it's in one of the bedrooms. There's a panel in one of the walls which is hollow and that can be opened by pressing the exact location. It leads through to the Tower going underground. Just think of all the work that would have gone into building such a tunnel. That must have been quite difficult hence the failed attempts."

They made haste in getting ready and set off for the rundown house which was now filling them with enthusiasm instead of despair.

On arrival they hurried into the house, making their way to the bedrooms. They almost ran but had to be careful on the uneven floor and the stairs were also precarious.

In the main bedroom they started tapping the walls but nothing sounded hollow. They looked at each other feeling discouraged.

Dale said, "I suppose we may have to face facts that it was boarded up centuries ago so we may never find it."

"Don't say that," said Clare despondently. "We have to find it."

They went into the next room and started all over again with the same result. Refusing to give up that easily Clare suggested maybe they needed to feel higher up and lower down the walls.

Going over it more thoroughly they continued. Dale being taller stood on tiptoe to reach near the top and Clare got down on her knees tapping the bottom.

Still drawing a blank they went back to the original room and tried again.

At first they got the same result until suddenly Clare gave a shout.   Dale rapidly went to her and crouched down to tap where she was. Sure enough it had a hollow ring to it. They looked at each other excitement shining in both their eyes.

"How do we get in?" Dale asked. "It definitely seems as if we've struck gold here."

"We keep tapping and when we reach the exact location it should open. It must be around here somewhere."

They tried tapping that area in minute detail until something started to shift under Clare's hand.

"We've found it! We've found it!" she cried with great excitement.

Sure enough the panel was moving very slowly until it revealed a dark cavernous space.

"What do we do now?" queried Dale.

"I don't know," she said.

"We could try going into it but we don't want to get stuck or anything. We also don't know how safe it would be. The tunnel may have broken down or may do so under our weight. It is centuries old after all," pointed out Dale.

"I don't know if I could do that. I want to look inside even if we don't go far."

Dale agreed they would try but was more cautious than his excited wife.

They went very carefully into the tunnel, discovering it to be solid concrete inside. They didn't go far as it soon got too dark to see and they hadn't thought to take torches with them. That would be for another time. What a discovery they had made.

. . . .

Once back at the house they headed straight to the bedroom and started tapping to find the tunnel opening. Finding it very quickly they stepped inside and switched on their torches, having decided two torches would give more light and would be better if the batteries failed in one of them.

Taking their time, they shone the torches all around the tunnel to see if they could find any turnoffs as they went along. There were lots of twists and turns but no other passages leading off in a different direction.

Continuing Clare and Dale made their slow way along the tunnel. For what seemed a long time they went downhill before struggling to go up. They came to a dead end. Shining the torches around they discovered what appeared to be some sort of trapdoor. They tried to open it but to no avail. It was completely stuck. They could only assume they had reached the Tower. They must report the diary and tunnel to the appropriate authorities as this was a piece of history and should be preserved as such

Gerbils

Hello to all who read this. You must be very careful to follow these instructions or it could be catastrophic for you. We are partial to a slice of finger pie occasionally.

When you first get us you must put us in a lovely large tank with plenty of bedding such as hay. Do not use anything dusty as it may affect us.

Make sure the bedding is nice and deep as we enjoy digging and making tunnels. If you are lucky you will see them as sometimes they maybe next to the glass. Be prepared to be amazed at our tunnelling expertise, but then, we excel at everything we do! Please remember when you insist on cleaning us out that we don't like it, you disturb all the hard work we have done and we have to start all over again.

We are lively animals and would love it if you take us out of our home often so we can have a good run around. We love a good party.

Supply us with plenty of cardboard for us to destroy in minutes. It is necessary for us to keep our teeth from getting overgrown. We don't like seeing the animal doctors when it could be avoided by providing us with chewing material.

Make sure you keep us informed of everything that is happening as we are inquisitive. We stand up on our back legs sniffing the air when we are investigating something that has captured our interest. We know you will find us super adorable when we do that. You won't be able to resist us.

We love sunflower seeds and peanuts. Give us as many as you want. You may hear that they are not good for us if we have too many.

If we stand near where the food is we want you to look for it as we will have kicked bedding all over it. Actually we are just being lazy as we could find it for ourselves really, but we are so friendly we love interaction with you humans.

Last but not least you should remember to spoil us rotten and let us get away with murder. It is mandatory that you fall completely in love with us, we can't help being so adorable and funny.

Mother Daughter Business

The rain was hitting the windows hard like stones. Such a dismal day, that hadn't let up since morning. They were stood together doing the washing up after dinner. The kitchen had a nice fragrance of lemon coming from the washing up liquid. They stood in a tense silence, mother and daughter Janice and Barbara. Janice was thin and tall, while Barbara her fourteen year old daughter was plump and short.

Barbara was stamping around the kitchen as she put things away, slamming drawers and cupboards as she did so.

"Come on Barbara the sooner you get this done the quicker you can go and listen to that noise you call music," said Janice.

Barbara remained silent just glaring at her mum. This was a nightly ritual over the washing up. It was always the same conversation. At least tonight Barbara hadn't dropped anything yet.

"Have you got any homework?" queried her mum.

Barbara shrugged.

Janice sighed, used to having a one sided conversation with her daughter. She supposed Barbara did her homework as there was never any complaint from the school.

Barbara picked up a wet plate and then crash! It slipped out of her hands irritating Janice who responded, saying, "Be more careful, can't you. You are always dropping things."

"You shouldn't ask me to do it then should you," said Barbara.

"Don't speak to me like that."

Barbara muttered something under her breath which Janice decided to take as an apology, whether it was or not. Barbara used to be such a nice little girl always polite and eager to help. She wasn't sure when it had all changed but now all she was faced with was a sullen, lazy teenager.

Barbara bit her lip, knowing she had to say something. It would never be the right time to impart this news but she had to get it over with. She tried to find the courage but somehow the words just wouldn't come. It wasn't that she was scared of her mum but she was unsure how mum would react to the news.

Taking a deep breath she said in a voice that came out as a whisper. Janice had to strain to hear her. "I'm pregnant."

"Oh darling," said Janice putting down the sponge she had been using and turned to her daughter.

Barbara burst into tears. Janice put her arms around her and held her close.

"It's Barry's I assume?"

Barry was Barbara's boyfriend of a few months. Janice hadn't been aware they had slept together as she didn't leave them alone together when they were in the house.

Barbara nodded, unable to speak through the sobs.

"It's ok darling, we can sort this out. When we have finished the washing up I'll put the kettle on. We can sit down and discuss it over a cup of tea," said Janice calmly, although she felt anything but calm. She felt angry and wanted to bang heads together but realised that wouldn't help the situation. Barbara was frightened and needed her support.

Barbara nodded but stayed in her mum's embrace not wanting to leave the safety and protection of her mum's arms. Eventually she quietened down and dried her eyes. They returned to the washing up, Barbara feeling lighter now she had confided in her mum. Janice with a heavy heart started thinking, wondering what they were going to do. What she did know was that Barbara was too young and immature to take responsibility for a baby. If she went through with the pregnancy it would be down to herself to bring the baby up.

Washing up finished and tea in their hands they went through to the living room to sit on the sofa to talk it over. Janice had her arm around Barbara in a gesture of support.

"Do you know what you want to do?" asked Janice, knowing her daughter probably hadn't thought it through.

Barbara shrugged and leaned against her mum.

"You are too young to have that responsibility. It's either an abortion or adoption," said Janice. She knew she was being blunt but wanted her daughter to understand the situation.

Barbara shrugged again. She was just overwhelmed by it all.

"Does Barry know?" asked Janice.

Barbara shook her head.

"I think we need to get together with him and his parents and discuss options properly."

"Do we have to?"

"Yes," said Janice, allowing no room for argument. She stood up and reached for her phone to contact his parents.

Janice didn't want to tell them over the phone so they arranged to meet the following evening. She felt sorry for Barry's parents who would be just as shell shocked as she was. She didn't know them very well so was apprehensive over their reaction.

....

They were seated on the sofa sipping tea. Barbara was pale and distressed ignoring her drink which sat on the coffee table in front of her.

Janice decided to get straight to the point. Nothing could be gained by putting it off. It wouldn't get any easier.

"It seems Barbara is pregnant," said Janice, not looking anyone in the eye.

There was a pause, Janice let the silence linger giving them time to take it in.

Alison looked horrified and turning to her son said, "What did you think you were playing at? When did it happen as you haven't been alone together except when you were out. I assume you weren't doing anything in a public place."

"What do you take us for? Of course we didn't," said Barry. "We went into that old hut on the recreation field a few times when it was raining."

"And one thing led to another," said Janice. "I think we get the picture. Why weren't you more sensible and use precautions if you really had to. I can't believe either of you were so irresponsible."

"We used condoms every time," said Barry.

"Every time!" Alison almost screeched. "How many times exactly are we talking about."

Barbara and Barry looked shamefaced as well they might. They were in a big mess and didn't know what to do.

Janice said, "Well since we find ourselves in this predicament we need to decide the best course of action. I have already suggested it is abortion or adoption. Neither of you are able to look after a baby and you have your future to think about, an education."

"I agree," said Alison. So far Brendan her husband had said nothing.

Barry stole glances at his father, worried. His father was strict and this silence was ominous.

"Can't you help us look after the baby?" asked Barbara tentatively.

"No, we most definitely cannot," said Janice, allowing no room for argument.

"We could manage ourselves," said Barry.

"You most certainly can't. Have you any idea of the work involved and the money needed to look after a demanding baby. You're too young to get a job."

Barbara and Barry said nothing.

"I think the best option is abortion then you can get on with your lives," said Alison. "You will never be allowed to be alone together after this. It's your own fault but it's clear you can't be trusted."

"It's a human being, I can't have it murdered," said Barbara finding her voice at last.

Janice was surprised, but inwardly pleased. It seemed Barbara wasn't as immature as she had thought and she was developing morals.

"It has to be adoption then. It would mean you would have to give it up immediately. I don't want you to have time to bond with it. It would be much harder to let go. I'm only thinking what's best for you."

"But I should have a say in the matter. It's my body."

"What is it you want then?" asked Alison.

Barbara sat in silence for a few minutes before saying, "I want to keep the baby. It's mine. I couldn't live with myself if the baby were adopted. It would grow up thinking it wasn't loved by it's real mum."

"There is a lot of work involved, sleepless nights, screaming babies that won't shut up however hard you try. It won't be easy by any means."

"I don't care. At least it would grow up knowing it was loved by its real mum."

"I understand what you are saying, but you need to be aware of what you are taking on. It's not easy with a new born baby at any age but you're still a child," said Janice. She admired her daughter, and was starting to come around to her way of thinking. Maybe between them they would manage.

"I think we need further advice," said Alison.

"First thing tomorrow I'll ring the doctors to have a chat through all the options with us," said Janice.

"Sounds good. Let us know how you get on. If you do go ahead with keeping the baby, Barbara we'll support in whatever way we can. I admire you for your thinking," said Alison.

They left soon after that and Barbara went into her mother's arms. "It will all work out you'll see," said Janice.

Sports Day

Ann cheered as she watched her small daughter running. It was the school sports day and Chloe was in the egg and spoon race and the three legged race. She was currently watching the egg and spoon.

It was a hot day, the sun shone, dazzling the eager parents cheering their children on. The sky was a brilliant blue without a cloud in sight.

Turning she spoke to her friend Adele, "She is way ahead of the rest of them, isn't she doing well."

She looked back at Chloe and screamed, "Come on darling, you can do it. I know you can."

Chloe ignored the shouts and cheers concentrating solely on the finish line which was fast approaching. She was well ahead of the others and hadn't dropped the egg once. She and her mum had talked about this and how important it was to focus on what she was doing and ignore everything else.

The finish line was in sight, as she edged closer and closer. Just a bit further and she would be there, an easy winner. She didn't dare risk a look over her shoulder to see where everyone else was. She just kept her eyes on the tape held by two teachers, one either side of the track.

Finally she crossed the line and the roar of the mums was deafening. She had done it. All that practice had paid off. She was the winner. Tired and with legs turning to jelly she sank to the ground.

"Well done," said her mum running towards her. "I can't believe it, my darling girl you've won."

Chloe was unable to speak, total exhaustion taking over. It had been quite intense for a six year olds body to take. She had enjoyed herself though. She watched the other children cross the line but was too tired to react in any way. Similarly, all those who had taken part were all exhausted.

Ann wrapped her arms around her daughter and lifted her to her feet. Chloe clung to her, tears in her eyes, a feeling of anti climax was taking over along with the tiredness.

"I did it," she whispered, repeatedly as if unable to take it all in.

"Yes my darling, you did. I am so proud of you. Just think what daddy will say when he gets home later."

Chloe smiled, she loved her daddy and knew he would be very impressed with her achievement.

In the three legged race she and her partner Louise were not quite so lucky. They were unable to get a rhythm going, therefore tripping each other up. This hadn't been like this when practicing but for some reason they just couldn't get it together. It was no surprise when they came last. They were disappointed but faced consoling hugs from mums who were proud anyway.

There was a chance of a brief rest before prize giving was announced. The children had been told they could put their hands in a bag and withdraw a prize. They were reaching in blindly so as not to know what they were choosing. When it was her turn Chloe went up to Mrs Bainbridge the headmistress. She put her hand in the bag and her face lit up as she clutched a small doll. It was wearing blue trousers and a blue and white striped top. She clung to it as she went back to her mum with shining eyes. This was the best day of her life and she couldn't wait to tell daddy all about it and show him her doll.

"What are you going to call her?" her mum asked.

"Polly," replied Chloe without hesitation.

Her mum smiled fondly at the small girl who was cuddling her new doll and talking to it, calling it her baby.

Mistaken Identity

She opened her eyes and squinted towards the clock. Jerking up suddenly she realised she was late for work, jumped out of bed, rushing for the bathroom. Elaine couldn't work out how she missed setting the alarm. She stopped and feeling a bit stupid went back to bed and decided to lay there a bit longer. It was Saturday, no work. How had she been thinking of work?

She lazed in bed, relaxed, wondering what she would do with the day. She had some shopping to do then maybe she and her husband could go out for a meal. Elaine reached for her phone to ring William. She expected him to be at work as he liked to pop into the office for a couple of hours on a Saturday while it was quiet.

No answer, how strange. He always picked up when it was her. She tried again but nothing. She shrugged, deciding she would get ready to go out before ringing again.

She dressed warmly, wrapped up in coat and a scarf as the weather had turned quite cold. As she rushed out to her car she decided to go to William's office instead of calling him again. It was only a short journey, easy enough to make a detour there on her way into the town centre. She reached the office but found it all locked up. Weird, she thought. Where could he have gone? It was normal for her to ring or pop into keep him company on a Saturday morning. He still wasn't taking calls.

She shrugged, sure there must be a simple explanation and drove off, intending to have a browse around the shops before going to Tescos to do her food shopping.

Elaine was in Marks and Spencer's looking at the warm jumpers when she saw them. She ducked behind a rail of clothes and peeped out to see more clearly. Yes, she was right. There could be no mistake, it was William with a lady. She felt herself flush with anger and something else which she couldn't identify. Without giving any thought as to what she would say she rushed out of her hiding place and walked rapidly towards them.

"Here you are!" she exclaimed. "I've been phoning you at the office then when you didn't answer I went there."

The man looked puzzled and said, "Sorry but do I know you?"

"Of course you do darling, it's me Elaine, your wife."

"Wife?" questioned the woman with him. "What is this all about Stuart?"

"Stuart? This isn't Stuart, he's William, my husband."

"No, he's Stuart and he is my husband."

"Ladies please, keep your voices down. I'm sorry, but there has been a mix up. My name is Stuart and I'm married to Linda here."

Elaine paled, starting to feel a bit unsure of herself. What was going on? He definitely looked like William.

"Lady, are you all right. Can we call someone for you? Your husband maybe?" Stuart queried, wanting to help. He didn't know what was happening but right now he was concerned for this lady who seemed a bit confused.

"No, no I'm ok. Thanks anyway, sorry to have bothered you."

She turned around and went on her way embarrassed. How could she have mixed him up with her beloved William? That had never happened before. There was an uncanny likeness though.

Deciding to abandon her shopping trip Elaine made her way home. Once back indoors she sat down looking up at the photo of her and William taken on their honeymoon. She smiled a sad smile. They had been so much in love. She reached for the photo album she left on the sofa the previous evening when she had last looked through it. All those pictures held precious memories of that short time she had with her beloved.

They had only been married a couple of years when William had been diagnosed with cancer. A year later his body succumbed to the illness and he died.

Elaine shook her head, allowing the tears to fall once more. How had she become so confused this Saturday morning that she thought he was still alive. Would this pain ever go away she wondered.

Beloved

He woke up with tears in his eyes having had a dream about his beloved Sarah. She had been there in her vibrant clothes of reds and oranges that she loved so much. She smiled at him, putting her hand to her mouth and blown him a kiss before turning and walking away. It was the same recurring dream he always had when he thought about her.

How he wished she had been with him. He still missed her so much. Maybe if she were still there he would have moved to the Promised Land or America. He still harboured a hope that if he stayed in Germany she would find her way back to him. Jacob knew it was futile but he couldn't accept she was gone from him. Sarah was never coming back.

She'd been the love of his life. They'd met in 1930 in Munich. Both being at the university there. He had been studying law and she history. It had been love at first sight for both of them. They had spent many hours together just holding hands and talking about their hopes and dreams for the future. They had married in 1932 when Jacob had qualified as a lawyer.

They were very much in love and settled down to what seemed a bright future. Everything changed however when Hitler came to power. First of all Jacob lost his job then they were limited as to where they could go. They had to wear the yellow Star of David on their clothes to identify them as Jews.

In spite of the hardships imposed by the Nazi regime they continued to be in love. They only had each other now as their friends started to shun them as it was no longer allowed to fraternise with Jews. They were now the underdogs, not fit to live in a civilised society.

Sarah and Jacob often talked of what they should do. They talked about trying to leave Germany but that fell through as they couldn't get the permits. They had left it too late.

It was in 1938 that things got worse. The SS were rounding up all the Jews to relocate them including Sarah and Jacob. They were shut up in cattle trucks with hundreds of others. They travelled for days not knowing where they were going. They were given little food and drink. Many of those who were weak and frail died on the way. The stench of urine and death was all around them.

Sarah and Jacob clung to each other desperate not to get separated. They didn't talk much, each terrified of what was to happen to them.   They were getting rapidly weaker and Sarah was sick frequently on the journey into the unknown.

"It's all right love," Jacob whispered to Sarah. "I'll make sure we stay together. It'll be all right." He was trying to reassure her as small whimpers came from her.

After what seemed like many days the trucks were opened and they were hurled out by men with guns. If someone was too slow or fell they were shot immediately. Jacob held onto Sarah, lifted her down and holding her upright. They had arrived in Auschwitz.

They were lined up and then men and women were separated into different lines. Sarah looked across at Jacob, desperation in her eyes. What was to happen to them? Would they ever see each other again?

They were forced to go in different directions. It wasn't until after the liberation of the camp that Jacob was able to find out what happened to his Sarah. She had grown weaker and weaker by the day until she was forced into the gas chamber and brutally murdered.

Jacob sighed as he remembered those awful days. The only thing that kept him going was thoughts of his much loved wife. He never got over those years in the camp, remaining physically and psychologically scarred. He looked at the tattooed numbers on his arm, a permanent reminder of what he'd been through.s

His Sarah was never coming home, gone forever, but he had loved her so much.

The Shopping Trip

"Come on you two, are you ready?"

"Aww mum do we have to?" complained Adam.

"Yes, you do. If you are good this morning we can go ice skating this afternoon."

"Yes," cried Adam and Rebecca in unison.

They could just about put up with shopping in Sainsburys if they could go ice skating afterwards. Quietly they put on their shoes ready to go. They bundled into the car and off they went.

Olivia sighed, she wished it wasn't so hard getting them to do the weekly shop. She was always having to bribe them. Last week it was ten pin bowling, this week ice skating. Without the bribe it would be impossible. They were good kids on the whole but passionately hated shopping. She supposed she couldn't blame them she had been exactly the same at their age. Anyway it was only two more weeks and then they would be back at school.

On arrival at Sainsburys they got out of the car and went into the shop. Olivia decided to split up the list and gave part of it to Adam and part to Rebecca. She would do the rest. The three of them split up and went their separate ways. At least doing this it would be over quicker.

Rebecca was in charge of dairy products so quickly went to where she needed to be to buy the milk, butter and yogurts. She was picking the milk up when she heard a voice calling her name. She turned and a grin lit up her face. "Josie!" she exclaimed. "It's great to see you. You mum's got you doing the shopping as well."

"Yeah, but I don't mind. I always have fun doing it. We make it a game to see who can do their half quickest."

"That sounds good. We have split the list up between the three of us but no competition."

"Come on then, I'll race you. How many things have you got on your list?"

Rebecca showed Josie the list and then off they went. Rebecca quickly grabbed what they needed in the dairy and then was off to the cold meat section for the ham.

Adam was dragging his feet, bored by what he called grown up shopping, but didn't dare grumble or they might forfeit the afternoon's skating which he loved.

It was his responsibility to pick up some cake and biscuits. Very unenthusiastically he went to the relevant aisles and put them in his basket. While there he couldn't resist the chocolate biscuits which he knew his mum would never allow. Looking around to see no one was watching he sneaked a packet into his jacket. No one would ever know. He had done it before and got away with it so was confident this time. If his mum found out she would kill him but he wasn't telling. He wouldn't dare risk telling Rebecca either as she was such a goody goody two shoes.

Shopping complete they met up at the tills. Olivia paid for it all and off they went. When they tried leaving the shop the alarm went off and a security guard approached them.

"Excuse me, I think you have taken an item and not paid for it."

Olivia was aghast, "There must be some mistake we wouldn't do that."

"I'm afraid I will have to ask you to accompany me so I can search your bags."

Adam tried to sidle away, still hoping to get away with it. Olivia saw him and his red face and realised. "Adam, how could you," she cried.

"I haven't done anything," he said sullenly.

"Empty your pockets young man," said the security guard.

Reluctantly Adam took out the biscuits.

Olivia was mortified, not knowing where to put herself. Everyone was looking at them.

"I'm sorry," mumbled Adam.

"It's a bit late for that. What were you thinking?"

Adam said nothing.

"Well that's your ice skating off this afternoon."

"Adam, now look what you've done. It's not fair that I get punished as well. You didn't think about that did you," said an indignant Rebecca.

"I'm so sorry for my son. Of course I will pay for the biscuits and I understand if you want to involve the police."

"I think I can leave it in your capable hands ma'am, but if it happens again we'll not be so lenient."

"Come on then you two, let's go," said Olivia grimly.

The Taboo Subject

"Can't you see what is going on over there! Why do you allow this in a public place?"

"I'm sorry sir, we didn't realise what was happening. I'll rectify this at once."

The harassed café owner went over to the woman sat at a corner table with an apologetic look on his face. "I'm very sorry ma'am but I'm going to have to ask you to leave. We've had a complaint from a member of the public."

"What? What about my rights and the rights of my baby who needs feeding?"

"I also have to think about my business and my customers."

"But I deliberately tucked myself away from anyone so that I could feed my baby discreetly without causing offence."

"I know, but I'm afraid there is nothing I can do now the matter has been raised."

The owner didn't know what to do. He was in quandary. On a personal level he didn't have a problem with feeding a baby, but he couldn't afford to lose customers either.

The mother stood up saying, "You haven't heard the last of this. You chose the wrong person to mess with. I'm a lawyer."

The café owner looked worried, but it was too late, too much had already been said. He walked away hoping she was bluffing as this could have a negative impact on his business if word got out.

The next day he found out what an impact his actions had. He was inundated with mothers and crying, hungry babies. They didn't even bother to sit in the corner but sat very openly feeding their little ones whilst talking loudly to each other and drinking their coffees.

He felt unable to do anything this time as they were in the majority.

The lady from yesterday had certainly been true to her word. His day only got worse when the local paper turned up wanting to do an interview and taking photos of the nursing mothers. Why hadn't he kept his mouth shut or stood up to the customer who had complained. He knew the type, if it hadn't been the mother it would have been something else wrong.

Seal Woman

The sky was dark with a brewing storm threatening. She looked back but she had no regrets about leaving. All these years she had spent longing to be with her real family – her seal family and now she must go back where she belonged.

Every night she cried herself to sleep at the loss of her real life, the life she had once had. A life with other seals in the deep waters. She never really understood how she had ended up separated and caught in shallow water and then completely washed ashore. Out of the water for too long had caused her to shed her skin and take on a human form.

She didn't see the life she was forced to lead as real at all. How could it be when she belonged in the water? She didn't fit in and didn't understand the human way.

As a seal she was a social creature living in a large family group of others, but now separated from them she felt awkward and vulnerable. Fortunately where she lived as a human was in a very isolated spot so she didn't have to communicate except with her human family.

There was a void, an ache, deep inside her as she longed for that freedom that the water offered her. She felt she was only playing a part, unable to be herself.

Her human skin was dry, parched, roughened like sandpaper. She wished for her seal body to come back, it was as if her new skin didn't quite fit.

With so many memories of her time as a seal, she hoped one day to find her way back. She missed the camaraderie she shared with the others in her family, all the games they had played, splashing each other, pushing and shoving and chasing as they swum rapidly. Swooping up and down and catching fish to eat.

She missed the cold, salty water that used to be such a big part of her life.

The man who had taken her in was kind and provided materially but it wasn't the same, she just didn't belong. He couldn't meet her deepest need.

She felt desperately alone. She often found herself standing at the waters edge, looking out to sea, wondering if she would ever enter that water again and be at one with it as she had once been. The longing was intense and filled her whole being.

She had tried explaining to the man but he didn't understand, he thought he and the children should be enough for her. Even after all this time she couldn't think of him as having a name and she never used it when speaking to him. In fact she rarely spoke. He often caught her daydreaming, in a world of her own. Sometimes she would have a wistful smile on her face as she remembered those wonderful times past.

Over time she noticed that her dry human skin was starting to flake away, very slowly bit by bit. Underneath was the fur like skin she was used to as a seal. She discovered that if she used her fingers she could peal more off. She stood at the waters edge one last time. Her face was alight with vitality and life again. The time had come for her to return to the water once more and become a seal. She didn't regret leaving the human life behind, after all it had only been borrowed for a limited period. The seals have much more fun anyway. Leaving her human skin behind she fitted back into the seal skin and waddled into the water where she quickly swam out to sea back to the life she once knew.

Trench Warfare

Arnold moved sideways along the trench filled with mud. He could hear his boots squelch as they went through the earth and water in the temporary lull in gunfire. All too soon the noise began again, deafening the men. He stood up bravely peering over the edge not sure what to do. He was in charge of these men but he had no training. There were no officers left with this battalion, they had all been killed last time they went over the edge into no mans land. The attempt to push the Germans back had come from higher up. Although the men knew it was foolhardy they had to obey orders or face a court martial.

Arnold came across Reg slumped against the side bleeding badly from a wound to his chest. He got a couple of the men to carry him to where the stretcher bearers would be able to get him to a casualty clearing station. Personally, Arnold wasn't convinced Reg would survive. Just another death.

Arnold had sadly become immune to the death he saw on a daily basis. It was just one more in a long line. It was all part of this existence in this terrible war. Like other young men he had joined up at the outbreak and thought he would be back with his family before he knew it. Not so, two years in and it was still going strong with no end in sight.

The cacophonous noise day and night of gunfire, the screams of the men when they were hit, the chatter going on around as they tried to keep their spirits up. It was never ending. Sometimes he just wanted to put his hand over his ears and scream and scream to block it all out. In his opinion it was hell on earth.

There feet were constantly wet from all the mud they were wading in.

Some of the men just couldn't take it which Arnold understood. They would have accidents with the hope they would be sent home. Of course if it was believed it was on purpose there would be a court martial for cowardice which surely would lead to death.

He moved back a bit to those who were resting, the men were chatting or writing letters home. In the letters they tried to sound upbeat to prevent worry from loved ones. They tried to prevent the chaos from getting into the letters but sometimes it was unavoidable. The death and the stench was unbelievable. They felt one had to be there to really know what they were going through on a daily basis

They were so tired having been there for more than a month now. They were due a rest away from the trenches but so far no one had come to relieve them so they stayed.

Seeing everyone was as ok as anyone could be under the circumstances Arnold had a sit down, leaning against the side of the trench. How much longer would this war go on for?

"Sir, sir," said a voice next to him, bringing him out of his reverie.

"What is it?" he asked sharply.

"Burt has been shot, he climbed out and they must have got him."

"What was he doing? I didn't give any command to go over the top."

"He was acting a bit weird sir, chatting about seeing his girlfriend. He said he was going to meet her and before we could do anything he had stepped out."

Arnold sighed as he got to his feet. This was all too common, men losing their mind and it sounded as if it had happened again. Not surprising under the circumstances with the conditions they lived in, the noise and lack of sleep combined contributed to it. When Arnold reached Bert he found it was too late, he was dead. This would mean yet another letter to his family to let them know what had happened. Of course he wouldn't mention that at the end he had been out of his mind. He would give the impression he had died bravely.

"Arnold, Arnold wake up. You've been dreaming again. One of your nightmares."

He opened his eyes and gave the nurse a sad smile, "This always happens around Armistice Day. What we saw, what we went through, no one should have to experience. It was supposed to be the war to end all wars but it wasn't. Those who died would turn in their graves if they saw the state of the world today."

The nurse nodded and tucked the elderly man in more comfortably. When she went to check on him later she found his eyes shut and a smile on his face. He was finally at peace.

The Scam

Adam turned over in bed and stretched lazily. He reached over to the girl and put his arm across her. She opened her eyes and looked at him. She couldn't even remember his name for heavens sake. How had this happened? What had they done?

"Hello, you're awake then," said Adam, he too couldn't remember her name or even if he had asked.

They had met in the nightclub and having too much to drink they had got together and spent the night at Adam's.

The girl got up hurriedly, pulling clothes on as rapidly as possible. She couldn't believe how it had happened. She looked around the room and discovered it bare except for a double bed with a cream coloured duvet and a wardrobe. She could see there was no other woman involved. No one would tolerate such a sparse room.

She went downstairs and discovered dishes piled up in the sink unwashed, confirming her opinion that this was very much a bachelor pad. The living room was a mess with papers everywhere. It looked like this man, whoever he was, worked from home.

Adam followed her down and asked, "Do you want breakfast?"

She shook her head thinking it better to decline for hygiene reasons. He saw her glance in the direction of the kitchen and gave an embarrassed laugh. "Yeah you could be right, not a good idea. Look I don't even know your name."

"Lucy," she said.

"Adam. How about we go and get breakfast somewhere. I really would like to get to know you better. I don't usually do this you know. Sleep around that is. I haven't slept with anyone since my divorce went through. I really don't remember much about last night."

She smiled to herself, thinking of the kisses, it had been wonderful really and she hadn't been as drunk as she made out. She had made a mistake in not asking his name though. It had just been a shock when she first woke up but now fully awake and aware of what had happened.

"Breakfast? I don't think so. I should just go." It was true she wanted to be gone and away from this man before he discovered his bank card was missing. She needed to go to the shops and then get ready to go out for the evening, ready to pick up another poor unsuspecting man. This is what she did on a regular basis and she hadn't been caught yet, helped because she changed her name and identity all the time.

Traffic Jam

"Oh no, look at all this traffic," I said.

We were on the motorway trying to get to the next town. Jane had decided it would be quicker this way. Big mistake! The traffic was queued up for as far as we could see. Definitely a few miles. It was at a complete standstill.

"We are going to be late if we don't start moving soon," I fretted.

Jane, still quite laid back about it said, "It wasn't like this when I came over or I wouldn't have come this way."

How boring. Cars with all different makes and colours. I suppose if I was interested in cars I might have taken more notice, it would have passed the time. It wasn't even the M25, notorious for traffic not moving.

If only I could read whilst travelling but I couldn't. I didn't want to be hit by travel sickness. The radio was on but I wasn't interested in what they were talking about. I wasn't even taking any notice. I was becoming so tense. Anxiety overtaking my body.

The traffic begun moving again and we inched our way forward ever so slightly. There was still no sign as to what was causing this tailback. Accidents, roadworks it could be anything.

Just in front of us I was suddenly blinded by this bright light. What was it? Where had it come from? It seemed to have appeared out of nowhere. I looked at Jane and she was quite clearly captivated by this brightness as well. I spoke, but she didn't appear to take any notice, it was as if I hadn't said anything.

I tried to shield my eyes against the radiance but to no avail. Was this the cause of the hold up?

I noticed a movement that seemed to be heading straight for us. This thing stopped next to my window so I wound it down.

"Can I help you?" I enquired politely.

The figure started speaking gibberish. All that came out of its mouth were sounds which to me made no sense. I was even more amazed when Jane turned and responded in the same way. What was this? I wondered.

Jane then turned to me speaking English. "We have to go with this thing. Step out of the car and follow the figure."

"We can't do that we are in the middle of the motorway," I said, astounded by what I was hearing.

"Just do it," commanded Jane.

Undoing the seat belt I got out of the car. The figure grabbed hold of me and forcefully marched me into the centre of the light. I was closely followed by Jane.

The light got brighter as I reached the epicentre.

"Get in," said Jane, her hand firmly on my back.

Having no choice I obeyed and climbed the steps I found in front of me.

Jane climbed in and helped tie me up inside.

"Stay still or you will loosen these ropes. It's a bumpy journey so you'll be glad of them."

"Where are we going?" I asked, very perturbed by this turn of events. This was like a dream from which I would wake up from in a minute, but it didn't happen. It was a waking nightmare.

I got no answer to my question. The figure couldn't understand me anyway and Jane chose not to.

We were off, we seemed to go higher and higher. Jane was right it was a very rocky ride to wherever we were going. There were no windows in this strange sort of aircraft so I was unable to get my bearing. The interior was a bright red colour with no seats we were just tied to the sides in some way. It was all very peculiar and that was putting it mildly.

We came to a shuddering halt. The small hatch was opened and I was untied and told to step out. What was this? I looked all around me and saw everything was red. No other colour was around.

"Where am I?"

"You are on the planet of the books," said Jane grinning at me.

"What?!" I exclaimed.

"This planet is full of books. I applied for you to visit here with the possibility of staying permanently if you like it. It's your Christmas present from me."

I looked puzzled.

"You love reading so when I saw this place advertised I thought it would be good for you."

I was too stunned to think. A planet full of books! All this from a motorway journey. Very bizarre, but I would keep an open mind.

I was guided off and taken along a pathway which I noticed was lined with books. So many, too many. I didn't think I would ever be able to finish all of them.

"I can see you like it," said Jane.

I nodded and picked up a book starting to read it.

"Yes, I think I will like this planet."

Together Forever

Flora looked across at her husband Tony with a grin.

"What are you grinning at love," he asked, turning the page of the book he was reading.

"Nothing really, just thinking. Do you realise we have been married nearly 30 years now?"

"Of course darling. I never forget our anniversary or how long."

"Yeah I know. You're not like Dora and Clive they never remember."

"I'm surprised those two are still together the way they carry on with their arguments."

"I know what you mean. I've asked Dora that more than once but she just shrugs. They are used to it and to change it would make them uncomfortable."

Flora and Tony sat in a contented silence each lost in their own thoughts. It had been a good marriage. Unfortunately they had not been blessed with children. They would have liked a couple, a boy and a girl, but it had only been wishful thinking.

What Tony didn't realise was that Flora had her own secrets. She knew why she had never conceived but she couldn't tell her loving husband. It would destroy them both and she didn't know how he would react. She would never get over what had happened. Neither the physical scars nor the psychological ones as well.

Flora yawned, "I think I'm going up, I'm really tired today for some reason."

"Ok, I won't be long dear."

She leaned over to give him his goodnight kiss before making her way upstairs. She wasn't really tired but the memories were really plaguing her and she needed an outlet. She went to the bathroom locking the door. She rolled her sleeve up and looked at the scar across her wrist. She had told Tony it had been an accident with a knife when chopping vegetables but that wasn't strictly true. A knife had been used, yes, but it had been deliberate. She had intended slipping quietly into oblivion, but it hadn't worked out like that, she had survived, waking up in hospital.

She reached for the razor slicing it neatly across the skin on her arms. Seeing the blood seeping from the wound gave her some relief. The problem was she didn't get that for very long and it was difficult to hide her self harm from her husband. If he were to find out what she did to herself and why, he would be furious. She was worried about what he would do armed with that knowledge. She didn't know why it was so important to keep it from him, she didn't care about the other party involved and certainly owed them no loyalty.

Flora covered her arms and went to bed. When Tony went to join her she pretended to be asleep, not wanting to get into a discussion. When she felt like this she just wanted to be alone in her own misery or she might reveal what had happened all those years ago. Finally she fell asleep, her lashes wet with silent tears.

It was while Tony was at work the next day she came to a decision.   She really couldn't live like this anymore, she had to speak out regardless of the consequences. She picked up the phone and made the call. She knew there would be loads of questions such as why had she left it so long to report it? There would be no evidence which would in reality make it her word against his. This had been building up for some time inside her, so her actions were not out of the blue.

Tony came home, bursting into the room, "You're not going to believe what has happened. Clive has been arrested. He phoned wanting legal representation," said Tony.

Flora paled, but wasn't surprised. Tony, so caught up in his story, didn't notice Flora's silence or her pallor.

"He has been arrested on suspicion of rape! Can you believe that?"

Flora sank into the chair. It was all over then, she thought. The words he had whispered as he raped her had stayed with her ever since. "We'll be together forever."

Finally Tony noticed his wife's reaction and sat down beside her. "What is it love, you're shivering. I know it's a shock but I'm sure they'll release him when they realise the mistake."

Flora whispered, "It's no mistake."

"What was that honey?"

Flora shook her head and said again, "No mistake."

Tony looked at her, and finally got the message. "Oh my darling! When did this happen?" He tried to take her in his arms but she resisted, knowing she needed to tell him what she should have said years ago.

Tony sat in stunned silence as his wife described her ordeal at the hands of their so called friend.

Tony fumed and said, "I'll kill him! I'll bloody kill him!"

Flora sat there rigid, surprised at Tony's language. He never swore, in all the years she'd known him not a swear word had been uttered.

"No you won't. You make sure he goes to prison and they throw away the key."

Finally she leaned against him and cried and cried as he held her close, never wanting to let her go.

Snow

Adele woke up and shivered. It was freezing. She turned to look at the time, it was already 8 am. She shook her husband Tom to wake him up. Fortunately it was Saturday so he got to have a lie in.

"Brr, it's so cold," said Tom. "I can't face getting up to that."

"I know what you mean but if we don't Wayne will be waking us up soon."

On that last word Wayne, their seven year old son, came running in shouting, "It's snowing, it's snowing."

Adele and Tom groaned and looked at each other. Adele got out of bed and opened the curtain a bit just to see what was happening. Exactly as stated by Wayne it was indeed snowing. Everywhere looked as if a white blanket had been used to cover everywhere and it was still coming down in big flakes. It looked so beautiful as it lay undisturbed by footprints or tire tracks. She guessed what they would be doing today. Wayne was going to want to be out there playing building snowmen and throwing snowballs. They had bought him a sledge for Christmas so he would be wanting to try that out in the nearby park where there was a small hill.

Wayne was jumping up and down in excitement. Adele and Tom looked on in amusement. It was as if Wayne had never seen snow before. Each year it was the same.

"Can I try out my new sledge today?"

"What do you say?" asked Tom, determined he should still be polite even if he was in a fervour of delight.

"Please."

Adele laughed and ruffled her son's hair. He was a good kid and they would have a fun day together.

"Ok, let us get up then or we won't be doing anything."

Wayne left them.

It was an hour later they were ready to go outside. They were all well wrapped up in coats, gloves and scarves. They walked to the park in the deepening snow. Tom carried the sledge for Wayne.

"Hey mum look at me," cried Wayne as he slid down the hill at some speed.

"Concentrate on where you are going."

Too late, Wayne came off the sledge. Tom rushed down but Wayne was ok, laughing, he had enjoyed his brief ride and was ready to go again.

Down he went with a scream of pure pleasure. This time he stayed on and didn't look back. Adele and Tom kept a close eye on him but he was fine. He climbed back up, longing to have another go. While he was on his way down Adele couldn't resist. She picked up some snow and modelled it into a large snowball which she threw at Tom. It caught him in the back. He squealed, turned round in surprise and saw Adele laughing. Realising what had happened he returned a snowball at her. She dodged to the side just in time and it missed.

"Just you wait," said Tom, "I'll get you."

He picked up the snow and chased Adele with the intention of putting it down her back. She ran down the hill where a bemused Wayne was watching his parents behave like a couple of children. Tom caught her up and shoved it down the inside of her coat. She shivered as it came into contact with her skin.

Wayne, not wanting to miss out left his sledge to the side and started throwing snowballs at his parents, who returned them. The three of them were having a lovely time.

Later Tom looked at his watch and said, "I think it's time we headed back now. We need to get something to eat."

"Oh dad, do we have to," moaned Wayne.

"Yes we do but there's always tomorrow. The snow won't have disappeared by then."

They went home where Adele made them all some hot chocolate to warm themselves up.

The Purchase

"Wait a minute, what are you doing?" asked Dana, horrified at what she was seeing.

"I'm putting the gerbils in a box, ready for you to transport home," replied the assistant surprised at being asked such an obvious question.

"But I reserved two gerbils."

"I've got it written down here as twenty gerbils."

"Twenty!" exclaimed Dana in abject horror. She was too stunned to speak for a minute as she watched all the gerbils being put in a box.

"I think there must be some mistake. I haven't a big enough tank or room for more tanks to keep them in."

"Oh that's ok. They sleep curled up on top of each other so don't require much space really."

Dana couldn't believe what she was hearing. Gerbils needed plenty of room to dig and make tunnels. Yes, of course she knew they didn't take up much space when asleep but they needed plenty of room for playing and going about their business. She didn't want them fighting due to lack of space, besides she loved her gerbils and wanted to give them the best life she could.

"What about all the space needed to play. They can't be kept in such a small area it's not healthy."

"Oh they'll be fine," said the assistant in an offhand manner. She clearly couldn't be bothered what conditions the poor animals were kept in.

"I will report you if you continue putting all those gerbils in. I requested two and that's all I am taking."

The assistant shrugged. She couldn't care less.

Dana decided to look around the rest of the shop whilst she waited for the mistake to be rectified and was horrified by what she saw. The condition of some of the cages was appalling and too many animals crammed into small areas totally unsuitable. She really wished she could take more but she just didn't have the room. She would speak to all her friends when she got home to see if they would buy some of the poor darlings, rescuing from the conditions they were currently forced to endure.

Checking she did only have the two she left the shop without another word. If truth be told she was close to tears at what she had witnessed.

Speaking to her partner later that evening he said, "I'm sure we could make room for one more tank. It won't make much difference after all. At least we will be rescuing them and know we can give them a good life here."

"How many more do you think we can get?"

"Let's work it out. We don't need that computer now that you have your laptop so we could put another tank there. We put a tank on the coffee table as well. That would give us another four gerbils – two in each tank. Or if we bought bigger tanks then maybe three per tank."

"If we do that there is a greater risk of them declanning later," said Dana, starting to get excited at taking in even more gerbils than planned.

"You have a point but we will manage somehow. Tomorrow's Saturday so we can go together and I can help you take everything out to the car."

The next day they left home excited at what they were about to do. They were both crazy about gerbils and loved the idea of making room for more. Fortunately, it was a different assistant who served them this time. She did look at them as if they were completely mad when they requested more tanks and gerbils.

The car was soon loaded up with tanks and gerbils and off they went taking the animals to their new home.

The Visit

"Oh no, here's trouble."

"What do you mean? When have I ever been trouble?" Lily asked with a straight face.

"Well, let's see, every time I come sthere's a new story of what you've been up to," said Ben, Lily's grandson.

"Ask the nurses, they'll tell you I've been good."

Ben tried to stifle the laughter that was bubbling up inside. His grandma was a hoot. She would insist black was white if she could get away with it. Always flirting with the male residents and staff. A right practical joker she was. Everyone that met the frail old lady loved her. Some of the residents were right moaners but not his grandma. Staff got irritable with others but not with Lily.

"Hello Ben," said Joyce, one of the nurses. "Has she told you her latest?"

"What now? She's said nothing, except to insist on her innocence."

"Innocent! Your grandmother, I don't think so!"

"Let's hear it then," said Ben, knowing he was about to have a good old laugh. He visited Lily once a week and always looked forward to it.

"Well, when I came in this morning to say hello and give her medication she didn't open her eyes. I thought she was still asleep so I left her and went to the other residents. When I came back she was still in the same position. Getting a bit worried, as this was so unlike your grandma I felt her pulse to make sure she was still alive. A pulse was there so I decided to let her sleep until breakfast was ready. I was creeping out of the room when she shouted BOO at me. I was so stunned I dropped the medication. Your rotten grandmother had been awake all along, she just wanted to get me worried!"

Ben burst out laughing. Only his grandma could come up with a trick like that.

"Well grandma, your protests of innocence don't quite stand after that one. I don't know how you come up with them I really don't."

Lily sat there laughing at the memory of her latest joke. "Yeah I do come up with some good ones don't I," said Lily proudly. "Mind you some of the staff need to find a sense of humour. All I get from some is tut tut."

"You can be sure we have a good laugh on the quiet Lily," said Joyce.

"Like yesterday she had been drinking Ribena before she went to the loo. She then complained of passing blood, so the carer came to get me straight away. I came running only to find your wicked grandmother had tipped some of her drink into the toilet to make it look like a dark coloured blood."

Ben sat there shaking his head. He really didn't know how his grandma thought it all up. When he left he would make sure he phoned his parents to let them know the latest. He had to share the laughter around so that others could enjoy the humour.

"That's not all."

"Oh no, what else? Do I really want to know?"

"I'm going to tell you anyway," said Joyce, who was thoroughly enjoying herself.

"This morning when she was sat in the living room, she got hold of a feather duster and used it to tickle poor Ned's neck. He kept turning around to see what it was, but of course there was nothing there, your grandmother was too quick to be caught. Ned kept scratching at his neck and turning around but nothing there. Ned complained about his neck so I agreed to have a look in all innocence but could find no reason to suggest why his neck was so itchy. It was only when I glanced up and saw Lily's eyes dancing with suppressed mirth that I started to realise she was involved somehow. She looked too innocent and was of course hiding the duster so I couldn't see it. I knew she was behind the irritation I just had to work out how. It was at that moment that the cleaner came complaining she had lost her duster that I realised how Lily had been doing it."

Ben roared with laughter, unable to contain himself this time. He never knew what he was going to hear next. He spent an hour with Lily before leaving, promising to visit again the following week. It was definitely something he would be looking forward to.

The Proposal

Jackie hurriedly got changed. She couldn't wait, she was going out with her boyfriend. They'd been going out for six months now.

The doorbell rang.

"Are you ready yet," called her mum up the stairs.

"Almost," she responded.

It was always the same. She endeavoured to get ready in plenty of time but still he arrived before she'd finished.

"She not ready again," she heard him saying. "She would be late for her own funeral and I hate to think how late she will be for our wedding."

Wedding? Had she heard right? Could he possibly be thinking of a future with her? In her excitement she rushed down the stairs in her slippers and was halfway out the door when she realised.

Steve shook his head in mock despair, she would never change. If truth be told he didn't want her to, he loved her just as she was. He felt in his pocket for the small box. Yes, it was there ready and waiting. First of all they were going to see a film then have a meal. It was then he intended to propose.

Once in the car Jackie chatted excitedly about her day. She hadn't been working so had been free to go shopping. She had been looking in jewellers at engagement rings in the hope that one day they would get married. She didn't tell him this part however. She was worried if she said anything she might frighten him off.

There was a sudden loud bang and then total silence. Steve lifted his head which had been buried in the airbag and looked at Jackie. She was leaning forward with her head on the dashboard and her eyes closed.

Oh no Jackie, his Jackie was hurt and he hadn't the chance to propose to her yet. He felt around in his pocket for his phone. He tried to relax once he knew the ambulance was on its way and he had phoned his parents and hers as well.

They all met up at the hospital where they all had an anxious wait. Steve had escaped unhurt but Jackie and the driver of the other car were in a bad way. It was thought that the other driver had a heart attack at the wheel and that had caused the accident.

"Mr and Mrs Hartley?" queried a doctor opening the door of the relatives room where they were waiting. Steve stood up as well. "I have to speak to the parents alone."

"It's ok Steve is Jackie's boyfriend."

The doctor nodded and bade them sit down.

"Jackie is unconscious at the moment. We have done a scan and her brain is swollen from the trauma. At this stage we are unsure when she'll wake up or what the damage will be."

Steve paled, "You mean…"

"There could be brain damage yes," said the doctor looking at Steve with sympathy in his eyes.

Steve groaned in anguish. "I was going to propose to her tonight. I'd bought this beautiful ring for her."

"Fingers crossed, you can give it to her when she wakes up," said the doctor.

What the doctor wasn't saying was that she might never wake up. She was in a critical condition. He recommended they go home as there was nothing they could do if they stayed. She wouldn't be awake before the next day so it was pointless staying.

Mr and Mrs Hartley gave Steve a lift home and said they would pick him up to take him to the hospital the next day.

Needless to say, they all had a sleepless night worrying about Jackie.

They arrived at the hospital the next afternoon and found her the same as when they had left. She lay still, pale and with her eyes shut. Her face the colour of the white sheet and hospital blanket.

Taking a seat by the bed, Steve took her hand and held it blinking back the tears. She looked so helpless, not knowing if he would ever get his Jackie back.

He sat there nearly asleep when he felt pressure on his hand. He looked up startled and saw Jackie with her eyes open. He grinned and said, "Hello gorgeous, how are you? I've been so worried."

"I've got a headache," came the whisper from the bed.

Mr Hartley jumped up and went to find a nurse.

"Well hello there, we were wondering when you were going to wake up. Can you squeeze my hands, that's right, can you feel me touch your feet. Good. Well everything seems ok but I'll get the doctor to look in on you."

A couple of days later Steve and Jackie were alone, Mr and Mrs Hartley had gone to the hospital cafeteria for a cup of tea.

"You know if you didn't want to go to the cinema you just had to say, you didn't have to go to these lengths to avoid it."

Jackie gave a weak smile.

Steve decided now was the time while they were alone. He took the box out of his pocket and got down on one knee. "Jackie, I love you so much will you do me the honour of being my wife?"

Jackie beamed and whispered, "Yes."

Steve jumped up and down. He couldn't believe it she had agreed to marry him.

"Well are you going to put the ring on then?" asked Jackie with a laugh.

The Paint

She gasped, struggling for breath. What was it that had such a smell to it. It was cloying, stuck to her clothes and worst of all it was caught in her throat. She could feel her tongue swelling up as she went into anaphylactic shock. She struggled in her pocket trying to find her phone to call for help.

There were lots of people around but they didn't even glance at her so there was no help to be had there. She managed to gasp the problem before she collapsed against the wall and slid slowly to the ground. People seemed to give her a wide berth as if she were drunk and she got some funny looks. There was nothing she could do, she could no longer say what the problem was. She hoped the ambulance would get there in time. If only she had been able to get out of the shopping centre before she collapsed but it hadn't happened. She wished there were warnings up about the smell of paint then people like her could avoid the area completely, but nothing had been said.

She felt herself drifting off as she continued to struggle to breathe. Her wheezing breath seemed so loud to her she was surprised no one else could hear it, but if they did she was still being ignored.

"Hello love, can you hear me, I'm Jane a paramedic and this is Paul."

Receiving no answer, Jane felt for a pulse. "It's ok, she has a pulse but it's very shallow. We need to check her pockets to find out who she is and if she has an allergy. This seems like an acute reaction to something."

Paul felt in her pockets, nothing. Jane looked in her bag and found a driving licence in the name of Julia, but no allergy card.

"Julia, Julia can you hear me?" Jane tried again to get a response. "We need to get her to the ambulance as soon as possible."

They rushed her into the ambulance and gave her some much needed oxygen. Away from the smell that had caused the problem and with the oxygen the reaction started to settle down and she started to come round a bit.

"Hello Julia, it's ok you're in the ambulance. We are taking you to hospital. You seem to have had an allergic reaction to something."

"Paint," rasped out Julia.

"Ok try not to talk. You should start to feel better now you are away from the paint. It must be difficult if you can't tolerate it. How do you manage when your own home needs decorating."

"Organic paint."

Jane nodded in understanding.

They soon arrived at the hospital and Jane was given the treatment she needed to really settle the reaction down. In future she would carry a note with her to say what she was allergic to.

The Access Visit

He woke up with a scream. Immediately Patsy was beside him, saying, "It's all right, you're safe, I'm here."

David was too scared at that moment, unable to take in what his foster mother was saying. He recoiled from her touch as she attempted to comfort him. He was eleven years old and had been with her and her family for six months. Prior to that he had been in and out of foster care. Most carers were saying they couldn't handle the nightmares, the bedwetting and self harm. Behaviours he exhibited as a result of the abuse he had suffered at the hands of his mother.

Patsy began to sing to him in a very quiet voice, in an effort to soothe the troubled boy. Usually this worked and he would fall back into a disturbed sleep. This would continue two or three times every night.   Patsy was determined not to give up on him which would, in her mind, only send things spiralling even further out of control.

She was just about to go back to bed herself when David screamed once more. This time he didn't wake, he was just crying out in yet another nightmare.

Patsy decided not to go back to bed but grabbed her pillow and a blanket and lay on the floor beside him, in case she was needed again.

It was unknown exactly what he had gone through in his short life, but it was thought to be horrific. Patsy wished social services would tell her, it might just give her a clue on how to help him.

Next day David's social worker phoned to say they were agreeing access with his mother.

Patsy immediately responded, saying, "I don't think that is in David's best interests. He already has nightmares and other disturbed behaviour. I think it will just make things worse for him. It would be more helpful if he could have counselling of some kind."

"I am sorry but I am the professional here and in my opinion it would be helpful to see his mother. She has requested it and it is her right."

Patsy shook her head and put the phone down after taking the details, but inside she was fuming. Why did social workers always override her views? She was the one that knew the children in her care, social workers spent very little time getting to know them.

When David got home from school she sat him down on the sofa and tried to speak to him about the access visit.

"David your social worker phoned this morning. They are setting up an access visit with your mother for next week."

David pulled himself away from Patsy and buried his head in a cushion, unable to deal with the information and wishing it would all go away. In his mind he had already been through too much and they still expected him to have a relationship with his mother.

"No! No! No!" he shouted before pulling up his sleeves and scratching and biting himself.

Patsy leaned over taking him in her arms to offer comfort and to stop him from taking his feelings out on himself.

"I'll be with you don't worry."

"That won't stop her, it never has before."

Patsy took a deep breath not daring to respond in case he was going to say more.

"I wish she was dead. It would have been better if I had never been born. If I have to see her I swear I'll kill her."

He stopped. The tears came. He sobbed and sobbed, crying out all the pain and anger against his mum that had built up over the years. Patsy held him murmuring into his ear occasionally. He clung to her as if for dear life.

Patsy was worried by the strength of his feelings and was determined that she would ring social services the next day and let them know exactly how he felt. Someone had to stand up for the boy and no one else would.

Unfortunately social services refused to take any notice and insisted the planned access visit go ahead. Patsy was so angry when she put the phone down. Who were they that they thought they knew best? How dare they trample all over a child's feelings like that! What they were doing was appalling.

Tuesday soon came around and Patsy managed to get a reluctant David into the car. She had almost had to physically drag him out.

Patsy felt terrible as she drove along, feeling as if she was betraying him. When they arrived he burst into tears and refused to take his seatbelt off and get out of the car. She had to reach over and undo it herself. David lashed out and started screaming and hitting Patsy around the face. Patsy said nothing, knowing he was totally unaware of what he was doing. If only social services could know what damage they were doing to this vulnerable child.

Patsy took David's hand and almost had to drag him inside. The social worker was already there and looked on with disapproval at the tantrum David had clearly had.

They were led into a small room where David's mother already sat waiting. "No, I can't go in there. I don't want to see her. Take me home please."

"It's all right love, I'm here, you're not alone."

David shook his head, pulled his hand away and launched himself at his mother. He pulled her hair, bit her and hit her before the social worker and Patsy pulled him off.

"You hurt me! You made me have sex with you! You hit me and burnt me with cigarettes! You told me you wished I'd never been born!" The list went on and on as David once he'd started couldn't stop. It came spewing out of his mouth.

The social worker gasped as did Patsy.

"I'm so sorry," said the social worker. "I really had no idea."

"You should have listened to me," said a stunned Patsy. "I told you he was refusing."

"I thought he was just being difficult," returned the social worker trying to justify herself.

"I will be making a complaint you can be sure of that," said Patsy.   "Goodness knows what damage has been done from this visit."

On arrival home David rushed up to his room. Patsy gave him a few minutes then followed him. She found him with a razor blade trying to cut his wrists.

"You don't feel better by letting that out then," she said quietly, taking the blade out of his hands.

David shook his head. "You should have left me alone and then I would have killed her."

"Would that have helped?" asked Patsy.

David shrugged.

Patsy sat down beside him saying, "I know you wanted revenge but sometimes going to extremes will only get you into more trouble. By pulling you away from your mother we were saving you from yourself."

The Verdict

"Foreman of the jury what decision have you come to?" asked the judge.

"Guilty my lord."

There were gasps around the courtroom. How could it have come to this? Now it would be a case of waiting for the sentence.

Ross was taken aback by the verdict. He had been so sure that the little toe rag would get off. As slippery as an eel that one.

Samuel had been up on a charge of raping an elderly lady when he broke into her home. He had also broken into a residential home for children with learning disabilities and raped one of the children. A nasty piece of work thought DCI Ross.

Samuel came across throughout the trial as a well brought up family man with two children and a wife. A person with some respectability, that the jury would probably relate to. Ross had made doubly sure the evidence would stick before submitting it to the CPS to be on the safe side. It was unknown why Samuel had committed these crimes as he gave no comment interviews all the way through. It was DNA that really linked him, although there was evidence he had used a condom on both occasions. A right scumbag was Ross's view and now he thought the view of the jury as well. Not the model citizen he had appeared.

Samuel's wife sat in the public gallery in floods of tears at the verdict, unable to believe her loving husband was going to prison for a long time. An innocent man!

The trial had gone on for a week in total. The defence had got a lot of evidence to point out what a wonderful person Samuel was as he worked as a district nurse. It was believed by the police that this was how he chose his victims. He could pick on the most vulnerable. They believed there were probably more victims that were unknown about.

"No, no, no, this can't be happening," cried Samuel. "I didn't do anything. You've made a terrible mistake. The real perpetrator is still out there free to commit these horrendous crimes."

"Be quiet," demanded the judge.

There had been no doubt in the mind of DCI Ross that they had their man but why was the big question. No one had been able to draw that out of him, not even the skilled barrister they had prosecuting. It had been difficult for the victims to testify as he had raped the most vulnerable of people who made very unreliable witnesses. All the child was asked was to point out the person in court who had hurt her.

It would probably never be known why, but it would always haunt the DCI. That was the only part of the case that bugged him still. The only twinge of unease about the case.

The only connection that had come up was that Samuel had visited both of the victims as a district nurse.

His defence had said how much he loved his job and how passionate he was. He had a wonderful family who supported him all the way through. When he spoke, he had a posh voice, nothing like what would be expected of a low life thought DCI Ross. It was just occasionally that slipped and he spoke with a colloquial accent.

"How could they have picked me out? They don't even know what day of the week it is," sneered Samuel suddenly. "I've been framed."

Ross sat up straight and gave his full attention to Samuel's outburst. Could he be giving away the truth now that the verdict had been given. Maybe he would let slip why he had picked on them. It seemed as if it was because they were both unreliable witnesses, being as vulnerable they were.

"Be quiet," said his barrister. Until that moment he had fully believed in his client's innocence but was now changing his mind. It had been a particularly unpleasant case and he would be glad to see the back of it.

There was an outcry in the gallery, all in favour of Samuel which was deafening.

"Order, order," cried the judge. "Samuel Maguire I hereby sentence you to fifteen years for raping an elderly lady and a child."

Samuel collapsed back and had to be hauled to his feet by the officers who were now ready to take him away.

The Cruise

Wow, this was pure bliss the sight before her eyes. The ocean all around her was a perfect blue, the sky above was another shade of pale blue with the brilliant rays of the sun shining down, dazzling her.

She was on a cruise, getting over a long illness. She hoped the quiet relaxation would finish the job. She hadn't done anything so far except sit in a chair on the deck and read her book. Perfect.

She was disturbed by the approach of a tall man who asked politely if he could join her. She gave a nod and a smile and then turned back to her book, not wanting to get into conversation.

"Hi, I'm James," said the giant bespectacled man.

"Louise," she said abruptly.

"Isn't this lovely," said James, not taking the hint that she wanted to be alone.

"Yes."

"I might have to get my paints out and paint the landscape."

Louise looked up from her book with a bit more interest, "You paint?" she asked.

"Yes, I love to dabble a bit when I can."

"I wish I could, but I was always useless at art. I admire paintings though. I'd love to see it when it's finished."

"I have to start first," laughed James. "But yeah, if I do it I'll definitely show you."

They sat in a companionable silence for a while and Louise went back to her book, still resenting the intrusion a bit.

"Do you swim?" asked James.

"Well yes, but I haven't for years."

"Never mind you'll soon get into it again. It's not a skill you lose. Why don't we go now?"

"I'm not sure I can, you see I'm weak from ill health. That's why I'm on this cruise, to try and seal my recovery."

Louise hoped James would go away, he was getting too inquisitive. She was a private person at the best of times and she didn't want to have to explain or justify herself to someone she had only just met. She was happy with her own company and so far she had been left alone.

"Swimming is a gentle form of exercise, it might do you good," insisted James, who just couldn't take a hint.

Louise sighed, realising she wasn't going to get any peace.

"Well I suppose there is no reason why I can't get in the pool even if I don't swim," she said.

This seemed to satisfy James who began to walk away towards the pool. Louise stood up and followed. She didn't have to change as she had put her swimming costume on, hoping to get a tan, to cover her pale skin.

She got in the pool, and sighed as the warm water covered her body. She decided to hang on to the side and have a kick about to begin with. As she kicked she watched James swimming laps. He was certainly an accomplished swimmer.

The pool was not exactly blue it was a turquoise colour, which was a lovely contrast between the ocean and sky.

She let go of the side and tried a bit of swimming. She found she was managing better than she thought. She just hoped she wouldn't pay for it later.

James pulled up beside her, "You are doing well," he said.

Louise nodded not having the breath to speak.

"What is your problem if I may ask?"

Louise felt cornered, she didn't want to disclose personal information to someone she had only just met but felt she didn't have a choice. "ME," she replied, head held high. There was still so much prejudice about it she was wary about his reaction.

"Oh no, I'm so sorry. I wouldn't wish that on my worst enemy. My brother has it and suffers terribly at times. He has to be so careful to pace himself."

"Don't I know it, but fortunately I'm recovering now, I haven't had a relapse in a year so I'm hopeful."

"Great news," said James enthusiastically.

Louise smiled at him, she was warming to him now. He seemed all right and very friendly. She really should stop pushing people away, worried about their reaction when they knew about the ME.

From that time they spent a lot of time together, chatting, swimming, eating. By the end of the cruise they were firm friends and knew they would stay in touch.

A Christmas Fairy Tale

Once upon a time there was a little boy named Harry. He absolutely adored everything about Christmas. He would start pestering his parents very early to put the tree and decorations up. He loved seeing all the adverts and use them to decide what he wanted for presents. Unfortunately he never got half the things on the list. This year he longed for a trampoline which he could bounce on in the summer or if it wasn't raining or snowing in the winter. He didn't play with cars very often being a very active child, always on the go. His parents tried to get him to settle down with a jigsaw puzzle but they never succeeded, after five minutes he would be bored and want to be moving again.

He had met Father Christmas and his elves but somehow it didn't seem right just seeing him at a grotto for a few minutes. It wasn't long enough to give his Christmas list. What he really wanted to do was see him Christmas Eve when he delivered the presents. His mum and dad had told him Santa was too busy to stay and chat at that time as he had to get to all the other boys and girls, but he still hoped. This was his biggest wish and it would really make his year.

It was Christmas Eve and Harry was sent to bed at the usual time although his parents knew he would be up at some unearthly hour in his excitement. There would be no rest for them after that.

Harry felt himself being shaken, he opened his eyes and there stood Father Christmas. He gasped in surprise, unable to believe what his eyes were seeing.

"Would you like to come with me on my travels?" asked Santa.

"Oh yes please," cried Harry.

"Shh don't wake your parents, this has to be our little secret."

Harry dressed up warmly with some help from Santa then he took Santa's hand and they left. Outside the front door was a sleigh with some reindeer attached. Santa introduced Harry to each of them in turn. They nodded their head at him in welcome.

Inside the sleigh Santa put a blanket around Harry to keep him warm as it was a freezing night and was going to feel colder as they flew through the air. Harry was beside himself, he couldn't believe what was happening. He pinched himself to make sure it wasn't a dream, but no it all seemed very real.

There were so many houses and Harry was allowed to take the presents in with Santa and arrange them around the trees. Sometimes there would be a mince pie left out and Santa would share it with him. He couldn't believe his luck this was a truly magical Christmas this year.

Soon they had finished having been to every house at high speed, even faster than the high speed trains Harry liked to watch. These reindeer were spectacular and Santa couldn't manage without them. Harry was back home in bed but couldn't settle to sleep after all the excitement.

Next morning he went to wake his parents up and told them of the nights activities. "Yes Harry, that must have been fun," they said.

Harry knew they didn't believe him, but he knew it was all true.

The Tower

The boys were highly excited about their upcoming trip to the Tower of London.

"Calm down you two," said Ruby their mother.

"Mum do you think there are ghosts there, of the people who were executed."

"I think you are getting a bit carried away now," she said, giving a laugh.

"But you don't know," said Phillip.

Ben and Phillip were fourteen year old twins. They had the same rather ghoulish imagination and this sort of trip was right up their street.

They could find intrigue in the most innocent of places so the Tower was definitely going to cause them to think of all sorts. They were looking forward to hearing all about the torture and beheadings that took place there.

"Ben, how about Miss Adler getting tortured and threatened with execution for working us too hard!"

They both laughed.

"You boys are incorrigible," said Ruby shaking her head. "Something you may be interested in is that great uncle served as a Yeoman Warder there at one time. You will hear all about the history of the Tower from the current day Yeoman Warders. You can find out all that stuff you are interested in. They should be able to tell you all about the torture and executions that took place."

"Maybe someone will try and steal the Crown Jewels while we're there. We might even be the ones to catch them and then we will get called to meet the queen and given medals," said Ben.

"I think it's really unlikely. If I was a writer I could get all my ideas for stories from you two with all the things you come up with."

....

"Ok you lot, make sure you all stay together and don't get separated," instructed Miss Adler their history teacher.

"We had this great idea last night. We thought Miss Adler should be tortured and beheaded here," said Ben.

Those who were in listening distance laughed at the remark. Miss Adler was a stern disciplinarian and was a bit stingy with her comments on homework.

"You're never going to believe what mum told us last night, apparently the Yeoman Warders that show people round and give the history of the place, well our great uncle used to be one of them," said Ben.

"Come on you lot, keep up I don't want any stragglers today," called Miss Adler.

The group ran to catch up.

"What about if we see any ghosts?" queried Phillip.

"I think that is unlikely, first of all they are not going to appear when it's daylight but also this is too busy with so many tourists so won't appear."

"Actually ma'am ghosts have been reported as seen by some of our visitors. They are thought to be some of the people who have been executed here. People claim to see Ann Boleyn wandering around. I personally have never seen anything so can't be sure. It's all hearsay really," said the Yeoman Warder responsible for showing the school party round.

"Did you hear that," whispered Ben. "Wouldn't it be great if we were to see something."

"Yeah but how are we going to do that?" asked Phillip.

"We have to accidentally wander off and find a way of hiding then we wait."

"I don't see how we can do that," said Phillip discouragingly.

"I'll pretend to trip and hurt my ankle as an excuse to get separated. You wait with me for a while then you leave me to rush to find Miss Adler during which time she will have got far enough away for me to wander off."

"But what about me? I won't be with you to see anything. I don't want to miss out," complained Phillip.

"Come on you two," called Miss Adler. "I said you all have to keep up. If you can't I'll have to have you walk with me. I have no intention of losing anyone today."

Phillip looked at Ben and nodded his agreement with the plan. So that's exactly what they did. Ben stumbled and fell and Phillip stayed with him pretending to help. He gave it long enough for the group to move away before walking slowly to catch up with the others.

"Miss Adler," called Phillip from the back of the group.

"What is it?" she queried in a no nonsense voice.

"It's Ben, he tripped and hurt his ankle."

Miss Adler sighed and moved to the back of the group. "Where is he?" she asked impatiently.

"He was back here somewhere."

They walked briskly to where Ben had been but by this time he was nowhere to be seen.

"I told you to stay together. He shouldn't be this far behind us. What were you two up to?" she looked at him suspiciously.

Seeing no help for it he confessed everything. Miss Adler pursed her lips. "Well let's hope he isn't too far away. This is very inconvenient of you both."

They found Ben hiding behind a pillar. He looked disturbed as they approached him.

"Well there doesn't look anything wrong with you. Hurry up we have to catch up with the others and for the rest of the day you can stay at my side. I will of course report this to your parents."

Ben and Phillip looked at each other. They knew they would be in trouble at home as well.

"Did you see anything?" asked Phillip in a whisper.

"Stop whispering you two. If you have something to say, you can say it loud enough for me to hear."

Ben shrugged, not wanting to give anything away. Phillip was left in limbo, he longed to find out but would have to wait until they got home.

The Night Before Christmas

"Go to sleep you two, or Santa won't be here. You don't want to wake up to no presents," said mum.

"No presents," cried Damien and Ben in unison.

Damien and Ben lay quietly in their bunk beds for a while, waiting for mum to go to bed.

Ben was the first one to break the silence. "Let's get up and go and creep downstairs to see what is happening."

They were being as silent as possible as they put their dressing gowns on. They started downstairs when Ben managed to step on a creaking step. They paused, listening closely and sure enough it came, "You two back to bed now," came the voice of their mother.

Her bedroom door opened and she appeared but Ben and Damien were nowhere to be seen. The creaking stair had opened up and apparently swallowed the twins.

They found themselves in a dark, cavernous space. It took them a while to adjust to the dim light. They moved further in as they got accustomed to the space. They wanted to explore this strange sort of cave. It had a very low ceiling but high enough for two eight year olds to stand up in. It appeared to be empty, they saw nothing as they looked around.

"I want to go back to bed," whimpered Damien, who was not as adventurous as his brother.

"Wimp," said Ben.

"I'm not."

"Then come on and stop moaning. I want to know where we are."

They continued to move forward looking all around them but saw nothing.

"I'm cold," moaned Damien.

"Oh stop it. We're not babies now."

As they walked onwards there suddenly appeared a bright light. They hurried towards it, even Damien cheering up now.

They left the cave and emerged into a brightness. They had to shield their eyes, the glare was so vivid.

They looked around and saw strange creatures dressed in green with funny green pointed hats rushing about. These tiny beings were too busy to notice the boys standing watching them.

"Hello," called Ben, the confident one.

"Yes," queried a small creature coming over to them.

"Where are we?"

"Don't you know? You are in Santa's grotto of course."

"But where is Father Christmas?" asked Ben looking around but not seeing him.

"He's very busy don't you realise. This is his busiest time of the year. He is out getting the reindeer ready to visit all the houses on earth."

"Wow," said Damien.

They followed the elf further in and discovered bright lights of all different colours. The elves were busy wrapping toys up and loading them on a trolley which another elf dragged away, ready for Santa to put them on the sleigh.

The boys just stood enjoying the hustle and bustle going on around them. They looked on in awe unable to believe where they were. This was going to be the best Christmas ever, to actually get to see this was a truly magical experience.

"Can we meet Rudolph please?" asked Ben.

"I don't know. I'll have to ask."

The elf disappeared for a while before coming back to summon the boys. "Follow me but we have to be quick, they are ready to get off now."

The twins had to run to keep up with the elf. He might only be small but he certainly moved very fast.

"Slow down," cried Damien breathlessly.

"No time, you have to hurry if you want to see the reindeer," the elf said without slowing down or turning around.

Damien stumbled and would have fallen if Ben hadn't caught at his arm. "Come on you're slowing us down," said Ben irritably.

Poor Damien was going as fast as he could but wasn't as strong or as fast as his twin.

Eventually the elf led them along a dark passageway. At the end they found a glorious sight. A giant sleigh stood there with reindeer attached ready to take off in the galaxy. In the sleigh there were brightly wrapped parcels of all shapes and sizes. They saw a large, rotund man in a red suit and long white beard. He had a beaming grin and a twinkle in his eyes. The boys knew instantly that he was very friendly and cheerful.

"Hello Damien and Ben," said Santa.

"How do you know our names?" asked Ben.

"I'm Father Christmas! It's my job to know the names of all the little children." He got out of the sleigh and went down on bended knee so he was at the same height as the twins.

"Would you like to come with me and I can take you home on my way?"

"Oh yes please," they answered together.

Santa laughed and ushered them on to the sleigh. They sat down and marvelled at the sight.

"Now hold on tight."

They clung to the sides of the sleigh as the reindeer ran and took off into the air.

The amazed and awestruck look on the boys faces told of everything they felt about their adventure. They couldn't wait until they could tell all their friends about Christmas this year.

All too soon the journey was over and they came to a stop outside the boys house. Father Christmas got out and going ahead of the boys he opened the door and let the boys enter before him.

"How did you do that?"

"I have a key to every house. How do you think I manage to leave presents for all the children in the world?"

The boys accepted this explanation and went into their house. Before going to bed they went into the living room and noticed all around the tree were lots of parcels. Damien rushed forward eager to see what was for him, but Santa held him back.

"Don't look now, go to bed and enjoy opening them with your mum in the morning. She will want to join in the excitement with you."

The Dive

He named the skeleton Blunt. There was no reason for that name it was just the first word that came into his head.

He looked down at the finds he had made. Paul was certain that Blunt had a malevolent look in his eye. Maybe he should have left it where it was, but that hadn't seemed right either. It was part of history surely.

Paul and his divers had found the remains of a ship on the sea bed. This was just one of several skeletons that had been clamped in irons on the ship, obviously a prisoner of some sort.

The rope coiled next to Blunt was new and signified what they found on the wreckage. The original rope was frayed and clearly fragile, brown with age and the effects of the sea. It was thought to cause further destruction to bring it to the surface.

A chest had also been discovered. It had something on it but they couldn't make out what it was. It appeared to be some sort of symbol but it had eroded over time. It took two of the divers to bring it up out of the sea. It was locked, so they needed to make another dive to hunt specifically for the key. Paul didn't know if the key would work, if indeed they could find it. The lock was brown with rust and surely the key would be as well. A week later the team make another dive to have a look, not only for the key but for anything else of further interest.

"You all know what we are looking for so let's not waste further time. See you back here to debrief later," said Paul.

The divers nodded in assent before they all went over the side of the boat. If their details were accurate the ship was directly below them.

Down and down they went each one focused on their job.

Back on the sunken ship Paul immediately got to work looking for any tiny thing that could resemble a key. The other divers were in different parts of the ship it having been decided to split the ship up between them. Paul loved being in deep water it was always so beautiful and he considered his job to be the best in the world. The ship itself was full of coral and loads of small fish swam about all over it, hiding from possible predators. The ocean itself was a beautiful aquamarine colour and clear, undisturbed in appearance.

One of the other divers went over to Paul holding a large key ring with a number of keys on. Paul made an o shape with his thumb and first finger to indicate he had done good work. Paul gave him the thumbs up to indicate he should surface. Paul however, stayed down wanting to investigate further. He had his suspicions that it might be an old pirate ship. He was basing his thoughts on the treasure chest and the manacled prisoners.

Later back on the surface on the quayside they went through what they had discovered. There were odd pieces of jewellery and a large iron ring with keys on it. As expected the keys were brown and rough with rust.

"Well come on then guys, someone try a key in the lock. I don't know about you but I'm excited to see what's inside," said Paul.

One of the divers stepped forward and tried one of the keys in the lock.

It turned slightly getting the others excited but that was it, no further. "This is useless, there is too much rust here," he said.

"Let's not give up just yet, it might just be the wrong key."

Dave shrugged and tried another one. This one didn't turn at all. He looked up at Paul who indicated he should keep trying. Putting the other key in the lock which was slightly smaller than the others they found it turned slightly. That was it no more keys and the lock still not open.

"There are either more keys down there or it's one of these," said Paul.

They all looked disheartened but Paul refused to give up. He took the keys from Dave and tried himself to no avail.

"These are too rusty. That lock isn't too good either," said Paul with a shake of his head.

"Here," said Dave, handing a screwdriver to Paul.

"What's this for?" queried Paul.

"I thought it might scrape some of the rust off to see if that would make a difference."

"Good thinking mate."

Paul worked away at the lock and the keys in an effort to get rid of at least some of the rust. He noticed that a bit of the rust did come off. Trying again he put the key in the lock and discovered it turned further this time. Excited, he kept scraping away until at last it turned and opened.

They gasped at what they found. It was a long way from the treasure they had expected – it was a human skull!

It was obviously very old but not as damaged by the sea as the other skeletons. The chest had protected it.

Paul shrugged and said, "I don't know what to do from here. This doesn't help solve where the ship came from or what happened."

"It could be a tribal ship that sank and the skull was the chief to preserve him for all time."

"That seems a bit far fetched," said Paul.

"Have you got any other suggestions?" asked Dave.

Paul and the others shook their heads. They were going to have to accept they never would know who they were or what happened.

Angel

Brett opened his eyes with a yawn. He hadn't had much sleep that night due to all the noise around him. The bed wasn't exactly designed for comfort either. The noise continued. It was always the same, 24/7. Sometimes he longed to escape the constant shouts and screams from those around him, in fact he longed to change his situation. He was living in a confined space the size of a small bathroom, there was only room for a narrow bed in it. It was very claustrophobic but there was nothing he could do about it. He was stuck there for the rest of his life unless the miracle he prayed for were to happen. He longed for a window to see out of but there wasn't one in this small space he called home, death row in Texas.

He had been there for over twenty years. Brett had no idea what it was like to be free as it had been so long ago. He dreamed of being released but had no idea how to function in a world that had left him behind, rejected and alone. The world had moved on he knew while he was stuck in a completely different era. He had no idea about all the modern technology which he knew now existed. He had a penfriend who talked of it all the time but he didn't understand what she was talking about. All that went on in his world was torment and nightmares, life and death decisions being made about him of which he had little say.

Yes, his lawyer was supposed to be working on his behalf but he didn't understand the legal jargon and ended up agreeing with everything that was suggested. After all what choice did he have if he wanted to get off death row. He had to trust his lawyer that he was doing his best but he found it hard to trust people, not surprising after what had happened.

He had openly cooperated with the police. After all he had been nowhere near the area where the robbery and murder had taken place. It turned out to be naïve of him but having had nothing to do with the police prior to this incident so was sure they would realise their mistake and release him quickly. He was a victim as well, if his car had never been stolen and used in the crime he would not even be in this situation now. They had stitched him up good and proper. He thought they would investigate and find out who did it but there was no investigation just them collecting evidence to prove he was the perpetrator.

Prior to this, Brett had been a plumber with a wife and two children. He had a good life, but how things had changed. His wife divorced him after the sentence was passed, not wanting to be associated with someone on death row. He hadn't seen his children in all that time either. He was totally alone except for his beautiful guardian angel Beth.

Beth wrote to him regularly from the UK. He loved hearing from her and hearing what was happening in her life. It kept him going day after day of the same monotonous routine. He was able to imagine her daily life through her letters and photos. She would never know how much her continued friendship meant to this lonely, frightened man. She would never know the terror he felt every day not knowing if the date would be given. At the same time part of him would be glad if he were to get given a date because at least he knew his torment would soon be over instead of being stuck in limbo year after year.

Just her describing the leaves changing colour and falling allowed him to go in his imagination to see it happening. How he longed to see a tree again.

The noise seemed to increase in the prison. There were screams from men who had finally gone mad and could take no more, there were men calling to each other from their individual cells. How he wished he could tune out for a while, peace and quiet would be bliss. He longed to have contact with another human being but that was never going to happen. His meals, if that's what they could be called, were passed through a slot in the door, no chance of any contact. If he were to leave his cell for any reason he would be handcuffed through that same slot before the door was unlocked. Brett had told Beth what it was like but he knew she could never comprehend the reality of his situation. It was a living death, pure hell, with no end in sight.

Yes, Beth was truly his angel. He appreciated her friendship so much. She would never know what a difference her life made to him. For that short while he could step out of prison into the real world, her world. It was like a breath of fresh air for him. Each day he longed for a letter from her and every time one arrived he couldn't help but spend the day smiling and reading the letter again and again. He wanted to soak it all up. He would look at her photo and think about his angel. The angel that made him smile, that was always there for him through the good and the bad. He felt he didn't deserve her but she continued to write never giving up on him. She kept him going when he would otherwise have given up. She lifted him up when he was down. A chance to escape his circumstances for a little while.

The Letter

"My dearest Emily, if you are reading this it means I am no longer with you. I suspect I did not choose to go this way but it was something long overdue. Please know how much I loved you. I don't know what you have been told but it may not have been the truth. It would have been fate calling me. I knew I lived on borrowed time, forever looking over my shoulder, waiting and watching, then running, but I could run no more."

Emily put the letter down, tears stinging her eyes. It was from her long dead mother. She had been packing the house up after her father had to move into a care home and had come across this letter in a box of papers. Why hadn't her father given it to her before? She was in her thirties for goodness sake. What did her mum mean? Her dad had said she died of cancer when she was four but according to this it may not have been correct. What reason would her dad have for lying to her?

Wiping the tears away she got on with the job. She slipped the letter into her pocket to be dealt with later. She'd talk it over with her husband and see what he suggested.

....

Brian looked up from the letter with a surprised look. "I don't know what to say," he said. "This does suggest something happened other than cancer, but what and why?"

"What do I do about it though?"

"The only way to start I suspect would be your dad but that would depend on him having a lucid day, and can you rely on him to tell the truth this time? If he has lived a lie for most of your life the chances are he will continue now."

"I wish my grandparents were around to ask. They might have known. It's times like this I realise how alone I really am."

Brian replaced his cup on the table and put his arm around Emily. "I'm here for you and you have my family, as big as it is, so you aren't alone."

"But you didn't know my family all those years ago."

"No but we can support you now in whatever steps you make to discover the truth. From reading this letter I suspect you might not want to know."

"I have to though. Don't you get it. I can't have peace until I find out the truth."

"I understand but it's all a long time ago and the truth might not be out there now. All you can do is start with your father and hope for the best."

Emily sighed and the tears started again.

"Hey don't cry darling, you're not on your own with this. We're in this together and we'll sort it out, whatever it happens to be."

She cuddled up to him, feeling the warmth of his jumper against her face and feeling the rise and fall of his chest which combined gave her a feeling of comfort.

....

It was a couple of days before she was able to visit her father. She just hoped today would be a lucid day. There was no way of knowing, sometimes he recognised her and other occasions he didn't.

She took a deep breath before knocking on the door. He turned his head but didn't acknowledge her, Emily's heart sank, it didn't look as if she would get anything from him that day.

"Hello dad," she said tentatively moving into the room. "It's me, Emily."

"I know who you are, there's no need to tell me," he growled.

She perched on the side of the bed and asked, "How are you? I hope they are treating you all right in here."

"What do you care? You never come and see me."

Emily bristled at this, but knew better than to comment. She knew as did staff that she tried to go in twice a week. He was just being cantankerous she knew. He'd always been like that though so she was used to it. His dementia hadn't affected that aspect.

"Well, what do you want?"

Emily sighed, she hadn't thought out what to say and what would be the point while he was in this mood.

"Well, spit it out girl. There's something on your mind."

"I read a letter from mum," she whispered, hardly daring to voice the words.

"Your mum," he yelled. "She's been gone years. Why bring this up now."

"I just found the letter in a box while I was sorting out your house."

"How dare you go through my things. I'm not dead yet you know."

"It….it was add….addressed to me," she stammered.

"But it was in my things which you had no right to go through," he repeated.

"She made me believe there could be more to her death than I realised. You told me it was cancer. Her suggestion though means you could have lied to me."

"So what if I did. It was for your own good. You are my daughter and I had to do what I thought was best and still do."

"But why?"

"It doesn't matter after all this time. She's gone and that's all there is to it."

"I need to know."

"No you don't. Now leave me in peace." He turned his head away indicating the visit was at an end.

Emily stood up with a heavy heart. She hadn't got any further and she had no idea what to do next.

Just as she was leaving the room he called to her, "If you must know she was murdered."

Emily stood still clutching the door for support. Had she heard right? Surely he was confused again. "What did you just say?"

"You heard! I said she was murdered!"

"What happened."

"It doesn't matter now it was all a long time ago."

Emily left the room and went home. Brian was waiting for her when she got in. She rushed straight over to him and went into his open arms.

"I take it you didn't get on very well?" he asked.

"She was murdered."

"Murdered! Are you sure? He's not hallucinating is he? It does sound farfetched."

Emily shook her head. "He knew exactly what he was saying. He refused to say anything at first then came out with it just as I was leaving."

"Well what did he say? Who did it and why?"

"He wouldn't tell me anything further, so I don't know where to go from here."

"I think we should look at the letter again in the light of this news and see where we go from here."

"Yeah, this makes sense now," said Brian as they looked closely at the letter. "It sounds like she was expecting something to happen."

"Hey look at this, it's a card from Auntie Jean."

"And she is?"

"She was mum's sister. But I don't remember her, I don't think mum kept in touch with anyone."

"We can believe that because she suggested in the letter that she had been running but I don't know why or who from."

"Here is an old address book maybe she's in there," said Brian.

"But it's so old she could have moved or died ages ago."

"Very true. It would be a starting point though."

Emily quickly leafed through the book until she found what she was looking for. She passed it across to Brian who nodded.

"I suggest we visit and see where that gets us. She can only shut the door in our faces."

They agreed to go the following day.

………

Emily gave a tentative knock and they waited. Emily could hear a vague slow shuffling towards them. A lady answered the door.

"Are you Jean Winslow?" asked Emily.

"Yes?" queried Jean peering short sighted at them.

"I'm Emily Dunlop. Carol's daughter."

"Emily, is it really you? I can't believe it. I haven't seen you since you were a baby. You moved away suddenly without telling anyone and leaving no forwarding address."

"Can we come in?" asked Brian.

"Of course, where are my manners." Jean stood aside to let them in.

When comfortably seated Emily got straight to the point explaining the letter. Jean looked wary making the young couple believe she knew something in spite of her protestations.

"I'm sorry, I don't know anything. We totally lost track of you when you moved without warning."

……..

"What now?" asked Emily, totally discouraged.

"I think we go back to your dad, only this time I'll come with you. As long as he is lucid he should be able to tell us everything."

They decided to go immediately. Fortunately he was very with it. Brian put the question to him, pointing out they had tracked down Auntie Jean.

"Why didn't she tell you?" asked her father.

"She said she knew nothing."

"What a big lie, she was caught up in it all. It was a big mess but the police had no proof so it didn't go further."

"Police, proof what are you talking about?" asked Emily.

Her father sighed, "I suppose I'll have to tell you. Your mother witnessed the murder of Jean's husband. The perpetrator threatened her, frightening her to the point we had to pack up and leave. Your mother never felt safe though, always worrying the murderer would find her. She did it to protect you as they were using you to frighten your mum."

He paused and Emily touched his arm in a gesture of support. She saw the pain it caused just by reliving it over again.

"Anyway where was I? Yes, it got to the point she was fed up with constantly moving so we stayed put at the last address, but she continued having nightmares and flashbacks over it. One day the doorbell rang I answered the door," he stopped abruptly as the tears ran unchecked down his cheeks.

"It's ok dad."

"It's not ok though. I've had to live with what happened next whilst protecting you from the truth. I let your Auntie Jean in. She grabbed you and said she was taking you away. There was a crazed look in her eyes. She had clearly lost the plot. When your mum tried to get you from her, your aunt pulled a gun out and shot her there and then in cold blood. Her last words were it was you. Jean bundled you into my arms with a warning to never go to the police or it would be you next. We moved that same day. I put your mum's body in the woods where she would be found quickly by dog walkers. I changed our names and invented completely separate lives for us, which included telling you a different story as to how you lost your mum. I have done everything to protect you."

Emily was in tears throughout the whole tragic story. Brian held her tight as she heard how her own family had been instrumental in her mum's death. She had one question however, "Who killed my uncle and why?"

Her father sighed and spoke, "It was Jean who killed her husband. She had been abusing him throughout their marriage and on this occasion she hit him over the head, he fell knocking his head on the corner of the table and never regained consciousness. Your mum had been staying with them at the time but had been made to believe it was an intruder who had done it as Jean had a black mask over her face and black clothing."

"We should call the police," said Brian.

"You can't do that, there is no evidence as there wasn't then, plus she must be getting on a bit."

"Thank you for telling me," said Emily eventually.

A Quiet Night in A and E

Amelia looked around her, all was quiet, too quiet for a Saturday night in A and E. She had just arrived by ambulance with a suspected blood clot. There had been a lot of whispering going on between nurses and the paramedics. Obviously they were all in the know. Being a rather inquisitive person, ok some would say nosey, she wanted to investigate, it would at least pass the time while she waited. She noticed something unusual from her position, no one else seemed to be arriving after her. In fact if she was right no one was leaving either.

There was something, although she couldn't put her finger on it. A shiver of fear went through her which she couldn't explain. Something was definitely odd here. She considered the possibility of trying to leave and see what happened, but maybe not yet as she wouldn't be able to find out what was going on and she was certain she had to know.

"Hello, I'm Doctor Schmidt."

Amelia started, she had been miles away trying to work out what was happening.

"I'm going to examine you then we can do some tests to see what is going on here."

She breathed in and out as required and allowed him to look at her legs, all seemed normal.

"We'll take some bloods and send you for an x ray but it might take a while as we are very busy tonight."

Amelia pondered his words which didn't make much sense. They didn't seem very busy, all was very quiet and staff just seemed to be standing round chatting instead of working. Something was definitely not right and she was determined to find out what it was. She worked out a checklist in her mind, listing a series of questions that needed answering. Now would she have the courage to ask questions of staff. Being very quiet, it wasn't really her style, she usually only spoke when spoken to.

"Excuse me, it seems very quiet tonight. Is everything ok?" she queried when a nurse went by.

"It's nothing to do with you," was the rather brusque reply.

Back to square one. Maybe she needed to be more subtle in her questions. How her friends would laugh at that as Amelia did not do subtle in any way, shape or form.

She tried again when another nurse went by.

The response came, "We are really very busy love, rushed off our feet, it is Saturday night after all."

Amelia thought about this. It was a strange statement considering there seemed to be nothing happening. She felt a flicker of unease. For the first time it crossed her mind that it might be a good idea to get out of there. If she left maybe she could get a taxi to a different hospital. She knew it would be pointless leaving and then calling an ambulance in case she got taken straight back. If she did this she would never find out what was happening but she had to think of her safety and she felt decidedly unsafe there.

Getting off the trolley she stretched herself, how uncomfortable they were. They really should get more comfortable trolleys for patients as lying on these ones seemed almost hazardous.

She walked towards the exit, trying to appear unconcerned. Staff seemed so busy in a huddle chatting that she thought she could get out unnoticed.

She reached the exit without being questioned, so far so good she thought. There were automatic doors but they didn't open as she approached which she thought was a bit strange. Never mind, she would try pushing but to no avail. It seemed she was locked in. The fear inside her intensified.

Amelia made her way back to her uncomfortable trolley without being seen.

"Excuse me, I think I need some fresh air," she called.

"I don't think that's a good idea, what if you collapse, it will be us that gets into trouble when we fill in the incident form because an accident happened on these premises."

"Please, it seems so stuffy in here."

"Oh ok. I'll have to stay with you though just to make sure you're fine."

The two women made their way to the exit. Much to Amelia's surprise the automatic door opened with no problem this time. It was very strange. Why had it not opened for her a few moments ago? Was it because she was on her own? Being with a nurse seemed to her a bit like a prisoner, it meant she could not escape even though she was now outside.

Amelia shivered.

"You're cold, I think we should get you back inside," said the nurse.

Amelia nodded, after all what had she achieved by this exercise? All she knew was that she could get outside as long as she was accompanied by a member of staff.

Once back on the trolley she didn't have long to wait before two men came along to take her to x ray. She smiled at them, slightly apprehensive as one of them didn't look quite right although she was unable to say what it was.

The x ray was done without incident but she noticed she wasn't being taken directly back to where she had come from. She queried it and got the response, "I know but we have a one way system operating when we are this busy."

"You don't seem very busy," responded Amelia.

"Just because it doesn't seem obvious doesn't mean we aren't."

Amelia nodded, although they had said nothing to allay her fears. In fact her anxiety rose a notch.

She was placed in a side room this time, apparently her place had been taken by another patient just arrived. She didn't believe this as no one had gone in and out while she had been there. They left the door open so she could see what was going on but it was all too quiet, eerily so.

Amelia didn't know how much time passed before someone came to take her blood. For some reason she couldn't explain she felt very frightened. Blood tests didn't usually cause problems for her.

She found it an unexpectedly painful procedure and the nurse showed impatience at the ouch she couldn't keep inside.

"The doctor will be in to see you when we get the results back."

Amelia nodded but kept quiet. She had a lot of thinking to do. She was still no further forward in solving the mystery that was taking place. She found herself growing very sleepy. She was too scared to allow herself to drop off but her eyes were increasingly heavy, very difficult to keep them open.

Someone crept into the room, Amelia opened her eyes and tried to scream. There before her was a giant of a man leaning over her. He was covered in hair.

"Wh…who are you?" she stammered.

"My name is Argie. I am here to take you with me. Your blood tests results show you are a suitable subject for us."

"What do you mean? I'm in hospital. I came with a suspected blood clot."

"We only take people with blood clots as you are a suitable candidate for our experiments. You were brought to a laboratory straight away and now we must transfer you to our planet for further experiments."

"When can I go home?" asked Amelia, knowing it was a some what futile question.

"Our planet will be your new home forever. You don't belong on earth."

Amelia screamed and screamed, hoping someone would rescue her. No one came.

"This is a futile gesture. There is no one around to hear you. Other subjects are in their own little rooms awaiting collection and all rooms are soundproofed."

Part of Amelia thought it must be a dream as she remembered falling asleep. Yes, that's what it must be just a nightmare that she would wake up from. It didn't happen. She was very much awake and it was all very real. A tear trickled down her cheek at the thought of never seeing her friends again.

"Come on we don't have time for tears, you are coming to our facility on our planet. You will be well looked after as we conduct our experiments into the human species."

With that she felt herself being lifted and carried away.

The Hat

"Do you remember that hat you loved so much?" asked the old lady.

"Of course. I loved wearing it, dressing up. I felt like a real lady in it."

She had been a child of six when she had found it in her mother's wardrobe. She had been looking for a pair of shoes that had a high heel to wear. At that time she had loved dressing up in her mother's clothes and that day was no exception. Instead of the shoes she had found a box. Taking the lid off she discovered a bright red hat.

The hat had captured her attention because of the colour, red was her favourite. Not only was it vibrant but it had different coloured bits of felt on it. They were circular in shape. Blue, black, yellow and green.

Claire had grabbed it and rushed downstairs to her mum, who had smiled indulgently at her daughter wearing that old hat. She herself had loved it as a child, it had originally been made for a school play she had been in. She had loved it so much she had kept it all these years and now Claire was having fun with it as well.

It was obvious it was homemade as it was quite amateurish in appearance. The texture was very rough as it had been made of papier-mache and painted red. To make it look a bit more professional it had a red ribbon around it.

Claire had been so enamoured with it she had wanted to wear it to school, but her mum had vetoed that idea straightaway.

"You can wear it when you get home if you want to."

She would often run around the house with her mum's clothes especially the high heeled shoes and that red hat. She couldn't explain why she liked the hat so much as it wasn't comfortable to wear being heavy and rough.

"You are so like me," commented the old lady. "I was just the same about that hat when I was young. Oh those were the days."

She stopped talking and a faraway look came over her and Claire knew she was going to hear more stories of her mum's childhood. Her mum couldn't remember recent events but loved memories of the past.

Boxed In

I am sat there on the ground waiting for someone to pick me up and open me. Surely someone won't be able to resist.

Ah, someone's coming, looks like a small being, surely they will pick me up and open me. I wonder what this small being thinks when they look at me.

I am small, rectangular in shape with red, black and white patterns. The patterns might make you think of old Aboriginal drawings but in fact they are the colours and patterns of the Shandians. I look as if I'm made of cardboard with patches of glue in places giving me an uneven feel. Someone looking at me might think I'm old and they would be right, I'm in fact over a million years old. I've been sent here on a mission.

Yes, the mini being is approaching, will they pick me up, will they. Come on, it's my time, yes, yes, you know you want to. I have been picked up but now I have to be opened and then I can begin my mission. I give a malevolent grin, which no one can see. At the moment all they see is an innocent looking box. The being runs off with me making lots of strange sounds. Unfortunately I don't understand the language of earthlings so I don't know what is being said. The being approaches a larger being and sounds very excited. The large being takes me and looks all over me then, yes it takes the band off which is around me keeping the lid on then, yes! The deed has been done I am open, we have been unleashed. Success for us but danger to earthlings and all they have known.

To anyone observing I look empty except for more cardboard with cuttings in it like sharks teeth. In those cuttings are small Shandians about to make their presence felt. I, of course, am the leader chosen to visit earth with a view to taking over the planet. You may wonder where I've come from. I came from the planet Shand dropped by one of our spaceships and kept hidden here on earth until the time was right.

The air that the small Shandians have been exposed to causes them to grow and expand. They start to slither outside me like snakes. The large being drops me as the Shandians appear and make their way outside of me, but it's too late the being is turned into one of us. You see, anyone who comes into contact with us automatically enters the realm of the Shandians where they receive training into our ways then will be unleashed on to earth. I, being the head Shandian on earth will oversee this. I will then send these underlings out on their mission to take over. I cannot fail, the deed will be done. In a very short time earth will be no more but an extension of the planet Shand. I will send these slithering underlings out on their monstrous mission to destroy planet earth. Whooshiaaawhoosh!

Unexpected Holiday

Michael looked furtively around. No one on the bus is paying him the slightest attention. He breathes a sigh of relief and turns back to his two small children. One is in a pushchair and the other is sitting on his lap, not much more than a toddler himself. The children look nothing like him, both having blond hair, he himself has black hair. He is going to have to rectify that. He can't afford anything that might identify them.

James and Nicky are good children on the whole for which he is very grateful. They love their weekends with him and start shouting excitedly when he arrives to pick them up. He ex bundles them quickly out the door, not wanting any prolonged contact with him.

This weekend is different he knew, although no one else realised. The children are excited about the bus ride. Usually they go somewhere in the car but today is different. Michael had plans. They are going to a nearby town and staying in the Premier Inn for a couple of days, he hadn't thought much further ahead than that.

"Daddy, where are we going?" asked James.

"I thought we'd have a little holiday," he replied.

"Ooh goody a holiday. Are we going to the seaside? I like the seaside but I haven't got my bucket and spade to make sandcastles," said the small boy.

"Don't worry we can buy another set when we get there."

James bounced about with pleasure.

"Sit still please," said Michael, turning and looking anxiously around. A few people were looking in their direction and smiling.

He sighed with relief when they arrived in Slough. They got off the bus and the first thing he did was go into a hairdressers to get the childrens hair cut, he would dye it himself.

"Where's the sand?" cried James, looking around.

"We're not there yet. Just a couple of days to go. Two more sleeps and then we'll go there."

He hadn't intended to go to the coast but seeing his child's excitement he couldn't resist. He'd give them what they wanted.

He hadn't really thought much further ahead than this. He needed to think and plan or he'd end up giving himself away. His parents lived in Spain so that would be an option, but not yet. That was bound to be one of the first places they checked and he didn't want his parents drawn into this.

Maybe a few days in Morecombe or Scarborough would be fine and then carry on north to Scotland. He had no ties there so he thought he would be safe enough. He intended growing a beard to make himself less identifiable.

Michael had become fed up with only seeing his children at weekends. He also knew his ex had a new partner and the children didn't like him. James especially was complaining that he would never let them do anything, expected them to stay quietly playing in their rooms. Claire, his ex, couldn't see any wrong in him so it was down to Michael to take action. He'd already gone down the obvious route of getting legal advice but his solicitor had said the courts always favour the mother and she would still get full custody. It had been then he had come up with the idea of not returning his children after the weekend was over.

"Daddy, I'm bored," complained James that afternoon.

They were in the Premier Inn and Michael was regretting not having made definite plans. He hadn't even thought about toys to keep the children amused. Nicky was fast asleep, thumb in her mouth. He sighed, they were going to have to go into the town centre and find a toy shop if James was to be placated.

......

When the children were in bed he logged on to the internet to google hotels in Yorkshire. He decided to take the kids to Scarborough for a couple of days. He also needed to get a rental car as he didn't want to be seen on public transport more than he had to, it would draw too much attention to them. He booked them into a hotel for four days on the seafront. According to the website the room would look directly out onto the beach. The children would love it and he found himself looking forward to it as well despite his anxiety that they would be discovered. He knew he faced arrest if he were found and he would never get to see his children. His ex would make sure of that.

The next morning he went to get the hire car and bundled James and Nicky into it. They set off northwards. They sang all the childrens songs they could think of to keep them amused on the long journey. Nicky soon fell asleep, lulled by the gentle movement of the car. James got bored and started protesting at the long journey.

"Are we there yet? How much further? I'm bored."

Michael started to get frustrated and didn't know how to keep James amused. There was nothing to look at out of the window except to see cars racing by on the motorway. No interesting views to keep a toddler's attention.

They stopped at a service station for lunch and a toilet stop. James became a bit happier now but Nicky was very grizzly having been woken up from a nice sleep.

It wasn't long before they were on their way again. Michael was beginning to regret what he had done. Suddenly he was no longer sure how long he could get away with it. What made him think he could do this. Their mother would be frantic with worry when they didn't turn up later that day. Was it really worth the risk of losing his children completely. He didn't want to see them for a couple of hours in an access centre somewhere with full supervision. He made up his mind and when they next stopped he took his mobile phone and made the call.

Lisa was surprised to hear from him and sounded upset. "Dylan's left me, he said he didn't sign up for children. He didn't want a ready made family. I knew he wasn't being fair on the children but I ignored it and thought he would come around eventually." She paused before adding, "Anyway why are you ringing? I'll be seeing you in a couple of hours when you bring the children back."

"That's why I'm ringing. I thought I'd take them away for a few days for a holiday. I miss them so much and have little quality time with them. We're on our way to Scarborough right now. If it's ok I'll bring them back in three days."

Lisa was taken aback as she had never agreed to this. "Well it's ok I suppose. It will have to be won't it."

Michael put the phone down. It felt as if a huge weight had been lifted off his mind. He had done the right thing.

It was a wonderful few days with his children. He gave them both the phone to speak to Lisa, which put the children in a better mood as well.

It was soon over and they went home, the children full of their adventures.

Hallelujah

Honk! Honk! The car behind started beeping, not surprisingly as we were in the middle of two lanes of traffic and were travelling at what can only be described as snails pace. I tensed up and gritted my teeth, anxiety taking over completely. Never had I known anyone drive so badly and I desperately wished I wasn't in the car.

"What are they doing, mad people," commented Clare.

I said nothing just continued gritting my teeth. What was there to say? She was the problem after all.

The car was a white fiat panda. The car reflected Clare's personality, worn out, torn padding on the seats and yellowing newspaper on the floor.

Oh no, a pedestrian crossing, there was an elderly couple about to cross thinking it perfectly safe, which it should have been, until bringing Clare into the equation who typically didn't stop but carried on driving. Heart in mouth and swallowing the nausea that rose inside at this blatant bad driving.

I wished again I could just get out, but it wasn't as simple as that. I was relying on Clare to get me to church, preferably in one piece.

A roundabout, I gripped the edge of the seat, wanting to close my eyes but not daring to. She slowed down, if that were possible. She slowly inched her way forward and I wondered why she was going so slowly. More honked horns. She was part way round when she almost came to a standstill for no reason, then she swerved and went over the raised hump that was the roundabout. Heart in mouth, I still said nothing.

"I stopped half round a roundabout once you know. I was unsure of the exit so I stopped to look."

I made no response except to nod, not trusting myself to speak. This statement didn't instil me with any confidence. I couldn't believe she seemed to be oblivious to her terrible driving.

"Look at those trees with all the blossom on. Beautiful."

We were approaching a junction and she was busy admiring the trees instead of paying attention to the road. This was obvious when she pulled out. Unable to keep my mouth shut I said, "You can't go, there's a car coming." My voice rose to a near scream.

This was a truly unbearable journey, one which I hoped never to repeat – that's if I survived this experience!

Hallelujah! It was with much relief we reached our destination. I got out of the car, shaking but in one piece.

The Session

"Ok in this session we are going to focus on the apple. You don't have to touch it but it would be good if you can."

Olivia looked at the apple as beads of sweat formed on her face. She started to shake. Panic broke out and she started hyperventilating. The seemingly innocent apple took on new tendencies in her eyes. It had grown horns and that evil looking smile were too much for her.

"It's all right, take your time. No rush. Try taking some deep breaths in and then out. Nice and slow now…. That's right, you're doing really well."

Olivia closed her eyes so she couldn't see the apple. This was her third session with the psychologist. In previous sessions they had just talked about her overwhelming fear of the fruit. It had taken a lot of courage to finally seek help as she felt stupid saying she had malusdomesticaphobia. She liked hearing the technical name for it. It sounded so grand.

"Can you open your eyes Olivia? Look at the apple, it's ok it's just sitting there, it can't hurt you."

Olivia shook her head, keeping her eyes closed. Nausea welled up inside and she started to retch. It was just too difficult.

"I've removed the apple now. You can open your eyes."

Olivia slowly opened her eyes and said, "I'm sorry I'm such a failure. I'll never conquer this."

"Yes you will," said the psychologist. "It just takes time. Do you want to tell me more about the time you last ate the apple. How did it feel?"

"I was only five. I could hear the crunch of it as I bit into it. It was quite tough, especially the skin. I thought it was pretty bitter to taste and it was quite dry inside. Not as juicy as some might be."

Olivia came to a stop, her face ashen.

"You're doing really well," said the psychologist.

Olivia opened her mouth but no sound came out. The silence was palpable as Olivia struggled with herself. She opened her mouth again but no words just the rasping of harsh sobs.

The psychologist sat quietly waiting for the storm to pass. He reached for a tissue and passed it to the troubled woman. The storm had been a bad one so it took some minutes before Olivia was able to stop with just the occasional sob catching in her throat.

"You find it really traumatic talking about the fruit. Maybe next week you might be able to take a quick look at it."

"I choked on a tiny piece of it and it got stuck in my throat. It was so frightening. I was unable to bring it up for ages, or at least it seemed like forever. I haven't eaten or touched an apple since."

The psychologist nodded before saying, "I think that is enough for this week. Don't beat yourself up because you couldn't look at the apple. We can do that when you are ready. There is absolutely no rush. I suggest you go home have a long relaxing bath to help you unwind."

Olivia stood up and gave a small smile as she left the room with a sigh of relief. The torture was over for another week.

A Life Worth Living

I looked at the pile of dirty dishes in the sink and sighed. Why was it always me who had to do the washing up with no assistance from anyone. It's like I'm their personal slave or something. Oh well, best get on with it, the quicker I start the sooner I'll finish.

Dishes done I started up the stairs to my room.

"Where do you think you're going miss? You haven't finished yet, I want a cup of tea."

I turned round and returned to the kitchen. I kept my mouth shut as I knew from bitter experience that saying anything would only make things worse.

Tea made and given to the rest of the family. No one was on my side not mum, dad or younger brother.

I made my way to my room, this time without being called back. I spent as much time there as possible. This was where I dreamed of escaping this drudgery and making a better life for myself. I sent a text to my only friend Melissa. She quickly responded with the suggestion we should go out the next day. I agreed but knew it might never happen, my family would never allow it, they'd keep me busy with something. So many times I had to cancel plans because of them. It didn't seem to occur to them that I needed a life as well.

I pulled out my notebook from my school bag and turned to the back page where I had notes written. These were my plans. I'd had to write in code because I couldn't be sure they wouldn't be read. Nothing was off limits with my family. We had learned all about codebreaking at school in history. If the workers of

Bletchley Park could break codes and keep their work secret then so could I. After all I didn't have to break codes just make them up in a way that I would remember.

There were a list of things: save pocket money, check prices of food, tell teacher and ask for social services to be involved. Going into care was just one option for me. I could officially run away and live on the streets, but that was bottom of the list as I wanted the opportunity to make a life for myself: go to university, get a good job, get married and have children.

I needed someone to take this seriously so at the moment I am contemplating the social services option. Maybe Childline would help, I hadn't thought of that before.

"Adrienne, come down here now," called my father.

"Coming," I responded knowing the peace and quiet was too good to be true.

Would I ever really get out? I have to, I can't take much more of this.

I made up my mind I would speak to Childline first and see what they said. I'd have to wait until I was at school the next day but that was fine. I just hope they will help and advise. I'd reached the end of my tether and I had to escape fast.

The Overthrowing

"Come on you brute. I'm in control here so you best remember that. You belong to me," said Nanita pinning me to the ground with her foot.

I give a little purr of submission but inside my temper is threatening to boil over. This situation couldn't be allowed to continue. I will speak to my friends and work something out. We are big cats, we should be in the wild not in this tiny cage with us all packed so close there isn't room to move. It's all becoming unbearable. How I hate being a circus animal. I want a better life. I've had enough of this.

My friend the tiger is now getting it. Nanita is cracking her whip and hitting him with it. He sits like a dog and begging, begging to be left alone more likely.

Nanita is wearing an orange skirt and blue top. Her long hair and the stern set to her mouth is enough to tell us who's boss around here. By rights it should be me as king of the jungle as I'm a male lion and leader of this group. I definitely need to rectify this situation.

What makes things worse is Nanita's hatred of us. She never shows us any kindness, always brandishing her whip. Well, no more, this will end one way or another.

When she leaves our cage we breathe a sigh of relief. At least we will be left alone for a while.

"Ok you guys, I don't know about you but we have to do something about Nanita. She needs a lesson in who is really number one around here."

The leopards, lions and tigers nod in my direction. We are of the same mind here.

"I suggest one or more of us create a disturbance and then the rest of us go behind her back and jump her. She won't see what we're doing, she'll be too busy brandishing that vile whip of hers."

"What will we do then?" asks the leopard.

"I suggest we maul her to death. It's only what she deserves after all she's put us through. That will be a lesson to anyone who thinks they can take over from her and control us. We must not accept control from anyone else. Anyone who tries it must be punished in the same way."

Nanita appears throwing in some meat for us. I attack my piece as if it was her. I tear the meat apart and eat. I just hope we are strong enough to execute my plan as she keeps us on starvation rations.

We are only here for one purpose and that's to entertain the crowds.

The time comes that evening just before we go into the ring. Nanita steps into the cage. I look at the others and we all nod in agreement. This is it then. Those chosen to disturb her do as planned. Those of us left immediately growl and jump her from behind. As agreed we maul her, tearing her limb from limb. We are so hungry we leave nothing to show she ever existed.

We get out of the cage which has conveniently been left open. Running through the camp we roar and run. It's hilarious watching the scared faces as they try to get out of our way. We make it to the ring where we go for the circus master. He suffers the same fate as Nanita.

It's over at last. After nine years of this we are finally free to do as we choose. We will never be caged again. Our life is just beginning. We smile at each other as we run off.

The Chair

The chair sat there, menacingly waiting to claim its next victim which would surely not be long in coming. It was placed centrally in a white, stark, clinical environment. There was glass at one side of the room ready for witnesses to watch the proceedings. For some it would be watching a tragedy unfold whilst others would be rejoicing, looking forward to the peace and closure they hoped it would give.

There was a permanent burning smell of death emanating the chamber which clung to everything and everyone who came into contact with it.

The next victim was Edward Bear, a serial killer of women with long hair. That had always been his fixation. If they didn't acknowledge him they would not survive. He was of a short stature which to those who had declared his innocence meant he couldn't have overcome these women on his own.

Edward was determined to go with dignity, the same way he had endured Death Row for over twenty years. He was ready, he had even given up on his appeals, feeling he'd had enough and just wanted this prolonged torture over and done with.

The murmur of voices could be heard behind the window as they waited for the condemned man to appear. In he walked, handcuffed to the men who would be responsible for the execution of this man. A palpable silence could be felt as he sat in the chair. He was fastened to the wooden chair with the leather straps round his wrists and ankles. He stared straight ahead, showing no sign of emotion.

Those watching felt cheated. They wanted some indication of fear that his victims would have felt as they died. They were doomed to disappointment. Edward refused to show any sign of the myriad of feelings swirling around inside.

He sat there rigid and upright strapped to the chair and waited. He   knew that for him there would be no last minute reprieve. It would all be over soon and for that he felt relief. His pain and suffering on this earth would soon be at an end.

He was asked if he had last minute words but he continued to stare straight ahead, giving no indication that he had heard.

The word was given that set the shocks going through his body. He jolted and shuddered as the electric current went through him. Then it was all over.

Those who had witnessed it felt nothing. The longed for peace did not materialise. There had been no friends or family to say goodbye to him only those whose lives had been damaged irreparably by his actions. They filed out of the room in silence overcome by what they had witnessed. The state had claimed its latest victim.

The Departure

Cathy walked up the tree lined road which was so familiar to her. She sighed, this would be the last time she would ever do that. She looked around at the familiar sites that lay before her. The neighbour out walking his dog lifted his hand to wave. It was a small, close knit community and she was going to miss it.

Her thoughts were centred on the row with her parents. She had known it would be difficult, but not as bad as it had turned out to be. She didn't know how they could be against Josh when they didn't even know him. They couldn't see past where he came from and she was automatically tainted because she had fallen for him. It was probably a good thing she hadn't had the opportunity to tell them his age as he was late twenties and she was only nineteen. She had screamed and cried and begged them to at least listen but to no avail. Her parents were not prepared to accept the situation and made it clear she no longer had any parents and they had no child. She hadn't even had time to pack. Her father had grabbed her roughly by the arm and pulled her out of the house and pushed her away so that she fell over. She sat on the gravel driveway, tears streaming down her cheeks as she looked back, to see the grim, stern set to her father's face and her mum in tears clutching her chest. That image would stay with her for the rest of her life. Her one regret was her dog, Charlie, the pair had been inseparable and now she had nothing and no one just the clothes she was wearing. She tried putting him out of her mind as he was part of her past now and her future was unknown.

She continued walking, having no money for the bus. She had no place to go except her boyfriend's house. She just hoped she would be met with a warmer welcome. As she grew nearer the more apprehensive she felt. She had never been there before. She had longed to meet his family and for him to meet hers but Josh had always evaded the idea, saying they weren't ready to take that step. She knew she felt more for him than he did for her but knew he cared deeply for her. She felt an overwhelming feeling whenever she thought of him. He always put a smile on her face. It hadn't been easy keeping their relationship a secret.

She finally reached the town where Josh lived. She searched in her memory to see what she could come up with as to the direction she should take. When she thought about it she realised just how little she knew about the area. Whenever the subject was broached he always managed to turn her mind from it and on to something completely different.

There weren't many people around to ask either, and those that were didn't look very approachable. She could see by the houses how rundown the area was and the few cars there were looked shabby and uncared for. Totally the opposite of where she came from.

She came across an elderly couple and thought they would be able to help. They gave her directions to the street Josh lived.

Apprehensively she continued on her way. She kept stopping and glancing around her nervously as the neighbourhood seemed to get rougher the further she went.

Finally she reached her destination. She stopped and looked at the house. It could certainly do with some painting but it looked marginally better than some of the other houses she had just past.

Her heart in her mouth, unsure of the reception she would receive, she opened the creaky gate, half hanging off and knocked on the door. She hadn't thought of what she would say when it was answered, she just waited. Maybe there would be no one in then what would she do.

She heard footsteps from inside, at least someone was coming she thought. A young woman faced her and looked expectantly at her. There was a toddler just behind, clinging to the woman's shirt.

"Um…um I'm looking for Josh," she said with a stammer.

"Darling it's for you," called the woman.

"Who is it? Tell them I'm busy," called Josh.

Who was this woman and why was she calling Josh darling, wondered Cathy.

"I need to speak to him, tell him it's urgent."

Josh came to the door reluctantly. His mouth hung open in shock when he saw Cathy standing there. There was something else unreadable when he faced her.

"Aren't you going to introduce us?" asked the woman.

"This is just someone I met once," said Josh.

Anger and frustration made Cathy burst out, "Is that how you saw it. I think we are more than mere acquaintances after all this time don't you."

"What does she mean?" asked the woman with a look on her face which didn't bode well for anyone.

Josh said nothing just looked from one to the other. Cathy was starting to make sense of the situation she found herself in and she didn't like the way her thoughts were going.

"You're married aren't you?" she said eventually. "And this is your child."

Josh said nothing just nodded, uncomfortably. He had never thought Cathy would come looking for him as she was poles apart from his experiences.

"Mum and dad threw me out when I told them about you."

"Why did you tell them? That was a stupid thing to do. You should have listened to me when I said we weren't ready."

"When would we be ready? We had been going out for a year."

"I think you had better explain," said the woman.

"There's nothing to explain darling. She just developed a crush on me and then started following me, turning up when I least expected it."

"What!" exclaimed Cathy. "That's rubbish and you know it. What about that afternoon we spent in the hotel room making love."

The woman turned and slapped Josh around the face. "How dare you! You've been having an affair all this time and I never knew. You've been playing me for a fool."

"I can see I'm not welcome here so where can I go? I can't go home."

"Not my problem," said Josh turning away. "I have a marriage to salvage."

Cathy stood there as the door was closed. She could hear shouting coming from within. She had no idea what to do. She had no money with her so couldn't even get a hotel room for the night until she could figure out what to do. She had a thought, surely her friend Melissa would help. Her parents were always welcoming whenever Cathy had been there.

She turned and walked away very alone and frightened.

"Come and sit down. You can't be running up and down the bus like that," Dan said.

Sam, his five year old son continued, ignoring his father.

Dan gave up. It was hopeless. His son was out of control and he didn't know what to do or where to turn.

Bethany was watching this and getting exasperated as the man was only half-heartedly trying to get his son to behave. It wasn't that difficult if only he were to try a harsher approach with threat of punishment. She wanted to go to him but ignored it as it was none of her business. The only problem she could see was the boy could get hurt if the bus were to stop suddenly. It was so irresponsible of the father to let him behave like that. It could also be a distraction to the driver.

She changed her mind and decided she would have to say something. It couldn't be left like this. She wasn't usually someone to poke her nose in other peoples business but she was concerned for the safety of the small boy.

"Excuse me," Bethany said having approached the man. "You can't let your son run about like that, it's not safe. The bus could stop in an instant and the boy could be hurt. It's also a distraction for the driver."

"I know, but I don't know what to do," said Dan.

"It's not that difficult. What's his name?"

"Sam."

"Sam come here," she said in a tone that allowed no room for disobedience.

Sam stopped in his tracks and looked at Bethany.

"Yes, come here," she said again.

He went to her and she sat him on her lap and spoke to him. "You can't run around like that on the bus. It's not safe. You could get hurt."

He looked at her but didn't say a word. He started squirming around on her lap desperate to get down. He didn't know this strange woman and was uncomfortable sitting on her lap. She held on to him tightly unwilling to let go.

"It really is this simple," she said turning to Dan. "Hold him firmly so he can't get down."

"He never obeys me like that. I can't get him to stop for even a minute," Dan said, putting his head in his hands.

"It's just a matter of discipline. Speak to him as if you mean it and he'll respond. He just needs boundaries."

"I haven't a clue what to do. My wife died recently. Cancer."

Bethany, despite her better judgement felt sympathy for the man. He was obviously struggling to cope and a hyperactive son wasn't helping.

"I'm sorry," she said, reaching out an arm to touch Dan.

To her horror she saw he was crying. Tears were pouring down his cheeks. She had a horror of tears and rarely cried herself. Her family and friends knew there was something serious if she were to cry. It was an alien concept to her. She was also uncomfortable being around others distress.

"When did you lose her?" Bethany asked.

"Two months ago," said Dan.

"I'm so sorry, that must be hard for you and your son," she said. "I'm Bethany by the way."

"Dan."

. . . .

"Hello Sam," said Bethany to the small boy who was now sitting quietly sucking his thumb.

"You saw how easy it is. That's all you have to do and he'll calm down."

"He's so hyper I can't get him to do anything. It doesn't matter where we are, home or away he's still the same."

"You have to be firm with him that's all. Speak as if you mean it."

Bethany was out of her depth. How was she to give parenting advice to a grieving man struggling to cope with his loss and having to look after a small child. She wasn't married and didn't have children. She was a teacher though and knew how to get obedience from the most wayward child.

Her stop was coming up and she was desperate to get off the bus and away from this sadness.

She leaned over and pressed the bell. "Anyway I get off here. I wish you the best of luck and hope things improve for you soon."

Getting off the bus she breathed a sigh of relief. That had been an uncomfortable journey. She couldn't help but feel some sympathy for the man who was clearly struggling. It was frustrating that he had no real idea how to get his small son to behave and showed little inclination to bother anyway.

Once home and the door shut on the world, Bethany felt she deserved a drink. Going to the fridge she poured herself a glass of red wine. She closed her eyes, that was better. Peace and quiet with a good book. That was her plans for the rest of the day.

Bethany soon forgot the encounter with Dan and Sam and went about her daily business. She was busy at work with marking and lesson plans to sort out. She taught the youngest age group with a mixture of four and five year olds. Bethany loved her work especially with this age group, they were so willing to learn. Much better than teens who just wanted to mess about and didn't seem interested in anything.

……..

It was several months later when she thought she caught sight of Dan outside the school gates. She looked again and saw no one so dismissed it from her mind. It couldn't be him. Why would he be there his son didn't go to this school or she would have had him in her class.

It was a few days later when she thought she saw him again. This time he was across the road from her flat. She stood watching him, trying to work out if it was him. How did he know where she lived or worked? She shook her head, it couldn't be him, just someone like him. He must be waiting for someone.

Days went by and she was becoming convinced he was watching her. He was turning up everywhere she went. He always tried to stay out of sight but there were still glimpses of him. She started to feel uncomfortable and didn't know what to do.

Over the period he watched her she noticed he was becoming more unkempt as if he was a homeless person. One thing that disturbed her was his son wasn't with him. As a single parent how could he not have his son with him. The impression she had of him on the bus was that he didn't have much support and was struggling alone.

Bethany wasn't scared exactly. He had seemed completely harmless on the bus but she was fed up. She decided next time she saw him she would have to speak to him and try and stop her from following her. She didn't know why he would. He hadn't seemed to be forming any attachment on the bus.

Her opportunity came at break time the next day.

"Hello Dan," she said.

"Oh hello," he returned.

"You sound surprised to see me but you have been following me."

"I haven't. How could I do that. I don't know anything about your life."

"Then what are you doing outside here. Your son doesn't attend this school."

"I…uh…often wander round on my own when he's at school," said Dan with a stammer.

"Yes, but it's always where I am which is concerning me."

Dan blushed, not knowing what to say.

"You were so kind to me on the bus. No one else wants to know me, they leave me alone now my wife's gone."

Bethany felt pity for him watching as his eyes filled with unshed tears. He was obviously lonely and had latched on to her because she had been kind to him on the bus.

"I'm not your wife though. I can't help you. If you're struggling I suggest you talk to your GP."

"There's nothing anyone can do. They can't bring her back. My son is a handful and I can't cope with his behaviour."

"Was he always like that or is it a recent development?" asked Bethany, suddenly wondering if it was the only way he could express himself over the loss of his mother.

"He's always been like that but has got worse since my wife died. She seemed to know instinctively how to handle him. To be honest I didn't have much to do with him as I was late getting home from work and he was in bed by then. I only saw him at weekends."

"What are you doing now? Someone must be looking after him while you're at work."

"I'm not working and haven't done so since her death. I can't face going back and seeing everyone feeling sorry for me."

"It might help if you did go back to work. It gives you something else to focus on besides yourself."

Dan nodded. "I suppose so," he said unenthusiastically.

"Well look I have to go. The bell is about to go for the end of break. Please think about getting help and try going back to work."

....

Bethany hoped that this would be the last of him. He didn't seem a threat in anyway, just a sad, lonely man. She was fed up of seeing him everywhere though. It felt like she was being stalked.

If she had hoped he would disappear she was very wrong. He was everywhere she went. He didn't even bother to hide himself now but did it openly. It was starting to get creepy.

Her friends told her she should go to the police about it, but she didn't want to get him into trouble. He was going through a hard enough time without them on his back.

"Hey, look over there. Your shadow again," said Jo, her best friend.

She glanced behind her and sure enough there he was. This really was becoming tiresome. It couldn't continue like this.

"Wait here," she said to Jo and she stood up and went to approach him, her face in a firm line of determination.

This was how she looked in her class if there was a pupil misbehaving. She stood no nonsense and she wouldn't with Dan either.

"What are you doing here? You're following me."

Dan blushed at these abrupt words.

"Where is your son? What do you do with him while you are out following me wherever I go."

"He's at home," said Dan in a whisper. He felt as if he was a naughty child caught playing up.

"Who's with him? He's too young staying on his own."

"My sister."

"But you've told me you have no support and now you have a sister to help you. You have to leave me alone. This can't continue. I'm not your wife or someone you can talk to."

"But you were so nice, I thought we could be friends."

Bethany shook her head. "No we can't. I hardly know you and quite honestly don't want to. You have to move on with your life."

"I don't know how," he said.

"Well going back to work would be a start since you have someone to look after Sam for you. This can't continue. I will have to take this further and contact the police if you persist in following me. It isn't normal behaviour and it becomes a bit scary after a while."

With that she turned and walked away without a backward glance. She hoped taking the tough approach would get the message across since he had ignored the gentle concern and helpful suggestions.

"Well I hope that's the last we see of him," she said sitting down.

"What did you say?"

"I basically told him it can't continue and if it does I would be going to the police."

Unfortunately, nothing changed. Dan was still everywhere Bethany went. She had hoped it would stop as she didn't want to go to the police but was starting to feel she would have no option.

He would presumably see her going to the station to report it, maybe that would deter him without saying anything, if he thought she were carrying out her threat. She hated the idea of reporting a sad, lonely man, but what choice did she have? She didn't like to admit that she was becoming a bit scared of him. Always there wherever she went was unnerving. Would he take things further?

....

Bethany and Jo approached the station. Jo had agreed to go with her for moral support and to back up what she was saying.

"Yes, how can I help?" asked the officer on the desk.

Bethany struck dumb by what she was doing said nothing. It was left to Jo who told the story as briefly as possible.

"Ok, take a seat and someone will be with you shortly."

They sat and waited in silence. They reception area itself was overwhelming and an air of authority filled the space. Bethany sat rigid and Jo wasn't much better. It had an intimidating feel to it.

It wasn't long before a policewoman approached and beckoned them to follow her. They were taken to a small room containing just a table and four chairs. Two either side of the table. It was dark with just one small bulb lighting the room.

They took a seat and the policewoman introduced herself. "Hi, my name is Melanie. Can you tell me what's been happening and I will make notes which you'll have to sign at the end."

Bethany gave an accurate account of what had been happening from the first encounter on the bus to the last sighting that day outside the police station.

"Well, it's possible he won't do anything further now he's seen you come in here. It might be enough to stop him. I will however type this up so it's on record. If it happens again feel free to contact me. I must warn you I'm not sure there is much we can do as he hasn't actually made any threat to you."

Bethany looked glum at this and Melanie hastened to assure her that it was being taken seriously.

They left the station in silence. Bethany looked around and sure enough there he was watching her.

He approached her and said, "You didn't have to come here. I only want to be friends. I'm not going to hurt you."

"But I don't know that," said Bethany. "To be honest I'm starting to be spooked by you turning up everywhere I go. It's time you moved on with your life. You've got a small child to think of."

"I can't though," said Dan.

"You need help," said Jo.

Bethany and Jo walked away without another word and got in Jo's car. Driving to the shopping centre where they planned getting a drink Jo saw him in the rear view mirror.

"I don't believe this, he's still there. Why won't he get the message?"

Bethany said, "I've had enough of this. So much for leaving me alone if it was reported. It's made no difference."

Bethany was getting quite frightened, not knowing if he would take things further and pose a threat to her. It was getting to the point where she was afraid to leave her house knowing he would be there behind her.

"I think I'm going back to the police," said Bethany when they were settled in the café drinking their coffee.

Jo nodded, "I think it's wise, he's not getting the message at all."

Bethany sat stirring her coffee staring into space.

"Earth to Bethany! Earth to Bethany!"

"Sorry I was miles away."

"No guesses on where you were and it wasn't miles away it was just across the road where Dan is."

Finishing their drink, they hurried to the car. They weren't in the mood for lingering as they usually would.

Back at the station they asked for Melanie. She came out with a smile. "I take it he's still there?"

Bethany nodded, tears in her eyes.

"Hey, don't cry, we'll sort this out. I know how frightened you must be. The fact that he hasn't done anything makes me think he's not dangerous just sad. Shall I go and have a word with him myself, it might get through to him if someone official speaks to him."

Bethany and Jo stayed in the station while Melanie went to speak to Dan. She was gone a long time which worried Bethany that she wasn't getting through to him.

Melanie came back with a frown on her face.

"It didn't go well?" queried Bethany.

Melanie shook her head. "He seems to know his rights and was almost laughing at me. He's an intelligent man and knows what he's doing. I think I'm going to look him up on the system out of interest. Sometimes this is a repeated pattern of behaviour and others will have reported him."

"What worries me is that he has a child. I'm unsure as to whether he has anyone to look after Sam."

Melanie looked serious, "We'll have to look into that for the child's sake. Wait here, I'll be back in a bit."

Melanie disappeared, leaving the two women looking after her.

"At least I can say life isn't boring!" said Bethany.

"Very true," said Jo.

"Although I would take boring over this any day."

"But what would we talk about?" asked Jo.

"We'd find something, we always do."

Jo nodded in agreement.

....

Meanwhile Melanie was becoming interested with what she was finding and it was grim reading. It appeared Dan had been in trouble for this sort of thing before. He had also taken things further with one lady and broken into her house convinced he had been invited. Who knew what he would have done next if a neighbour hadn't seen him and called the police. He wasn't the sad, lonely man they thought him. He really was a threat to women. He used the same story as he had with Bethany to get their sympathy. Speaking to her sergeant she agreed to arrest him and interview him to see what they could get out of him. Melanie was determined he should be stopped in his tracks before going further.

In reception once again, she told the two ladies what she had discovered but didn't say he had taken things further than just stalking. She said what she had planned to do and suggested they leave once he had been taken in.

"Another thought I had, could you get away for a few days. It would be best to leave while we are holding him which may only be a few hours realistically."

Bethany shook her head, "I'm a teacher so I can't get away during term time. If I went away for the weekend he would soon find me at school on Monday."

"That's a pity but I understand," said Melanie.

The two friends waited until Dan was inside before leaving.

"I think we should take the opportunity to go somewhere further afield for the day. He won't be able to trace you then, at least not until tomorrow."

"I'm not planning on going anywhere tomorrow so he'll have a boring day watching my flat."

"He doesn't seem to find it boring. He's just weird with fixations on women. At least though we know he has done this before and used the same story as he did to you. For all we know he may not even have a child."

"I hadn't thought of that."

"Well I only did when Melanie said he's used this story before to get sympathy."

There was silence for a while as Jo drove. They were going through lovely countryside but Bethany took no notice, she was too worried.

"I've had an idea," said Jo afterwards. "Why don't I stay with you for a week or so. If he sees you're not alone he might forget about you."

"That's a thought. At least I would feel safer knowing I'm not alone. We would have to make it obvious that you're with me though."

"We can do that. We can turn around now and go to my house to pick up a few things."

"No. Continue as we are. We might as well have some fun knowing I am free for a few hours at least."

Jo agreed.

They spent time browsing in the shops, just wandering around. Bethany felt more relaxed than she had for a long time. To be free of her constant shadow was a wonderful feeling. She hoped the police would get through to him so he would leave her alone in future.

They were laughing and chatting as if everything were normal. It soon came time to go back. The tension came back into Bethany and she grew quiet her jaw aching from gritting her teeth so badly, a habit she had when anxiety struck as it did now.

Jo glanced at her but didn't know what to say. Neither of them knew what they would be going back to. Would Dan disappear or would he ignore the police warning?

…………..

Next day when they got up Jo offered to give Bethany a lift to school instead of Bethany going alone. There was no sign of Dan as yet, but Jo didn't want to take any chances. Bethany gratefully accepted the lift as she still felt a bit shaky and didn't believe it was all over. It couldn't be so simple. Nothing had worked as yet so why would he stop now. Bethany thought he would only disappear if he were charged with something but that was unlikely to happen any time soon.

All through the day Bethany repeatedly looked out of the window expecting to see Dan in his usual place just outside the school gates. No one was there. She almost dared hope it was all over.

"Well, that was a relief to have no one there waiting," said Bethany when Jo was driving them both home after the school closed.

"I was sat watching all day and he didn't appear. Let's hope that's the last we see of him," said Jo.

Getting home Bethany stopped short of the front door.

"What is it?" asked Jo.

"I don't know, something doesn't feel right."

"You're imagining it. After all you've been through the last few months it's not surprising."

"No, you don't understand he's in there. I know it."

"How could he have got in? There are no signs of a break in. You're just on edge still. I'm sure there's nothing to worry about. He's gone," said Jo, wanting to reassure her friend.

Bethany shook her head. "I don't think so. It's a feeling I've got in my gut."

"Give me the key and let me go in first, we can't do anything until we know for certain. We would look incredibly stupid ringing the police and he isn't there."

Reluctantly Bethany gave Jo the key. Jo opened the door and stepped inside. She looked round the area just inside the door and saw no one.

She turned and beckoned Bethany to follow when Dan appeared from behind her grabbing her. He clamped his hand over her mouth to avoid any noise. With his other hand he tried to get Bethany in. Bethany was too fast though and turned, running in the other direction. When she was far enough away she phoned the police and reported what had happened.

She stayed at the end of the road having been told not to approach her house.

Meanwhile, Dan had Jo hostage. "This was all your fault. If you hadn't made her go to the police I wouldn't have had to force my way in."

"You couldn't continue following her it was starting to become threatening."

"I'd never hurt her. I wanted her to like me. I'm sure if given the chance to get to know me we could have been together," said Dan.

"That's not the way to get to know someone though. You can't keep following her."

…………..

It wasn't long before two police cars drew up beside Bethany. She quickly told them what had happened. They insisted she stay well back while they approached and tried talking him out.

"Hello, can you hear me? Is everything all right in there," called one of the officers through the letterbox.

There was silence.

"Hello, we know you're in there. It would be best if you came out now and we can have a chat. You know you are frightening the two ladies."

Nothing.

"Is Jo all right Dan?"

It was as if they were calling to an empty house as they continued to get no response.

"Come on you can't keep this up. It will be better if you come out now instead of making us come into you."

Another officer tried looking through the window to see what he could see. Nothing.

Walking back to Bethany one asked, "Is there another entrance as we aren't getting anywhere. We can't see what's going on either."

"Yes the patio doors at the back. You need to go down the alleyway and turn left at the end. I'm the first gate you come to," said Bethany.

The officer ran back to those waiting at the house. While two stayed at the front the other two went round the back, following Bethany's instructions.

They peered in the window and saw Jo sitting in a dining chair while Dan stood behind her with a knife at her throat.

Taking in the situation at a glance the officers quietly withdrew. It was a hostage situation and they needed backup. They deliberately kept this from Bethany just telling her they needed reinforcements.

It was another fifteen minutes before they arrived. Taking control a senior officer tried talking Dan out but continued to get no response. With officers surrounding the property they knew there was no way Dan could escape. The difficulty was getting Jo out safely. They had no idea how far Dan was prepared to go but they weren't taking any chances.

Bethany fed up with waiting, approached, "Can I help? It's me he wants not my friend."

"You need to stay back. It's not safe. We're working on it."

"You don't understand. He might listen to me."

The officer shrugged, "Well I suppose it can't hurt."

He made room for her by the letter box and she knelt down and called, "Dan, it's me Bethany. Why don't you come out and we can talk. You don't want Jo, so let her out. It's me you're interested in. I'm not cross with you. I want to know you and Jo are all right."

There was continued silence then a faint voice could be heard. "I'm not coming out. If I do they'll make me go back to that place and I can't. I just can't."

"What place Dan?" asked Bethany.

"It was a secure psychiatric unit."

"Maybe that's something you can negotiate when you come out."

Bethany looked at the officers who shrugged. They were unaware of his history as they had responded to the call. One of them moved away to radio the station to find out more details about Dan.

He looked serious as he listened and kept looking at Bethany. He switched the radio off and looked sober.

"Apparently he has done this before. He had a psychiatric assessment and was deemed unfit to stand trial. He was sent to a secure unit as he already said. He was let out at the beginning of this year."

Bethany looked horrified. "Will he hurt Jo?" she asked.

"I don't know," said the officer honestly.

There was a sound from inside and then the door opened. It was Dan, apparently deciding to come out. The officers took both arms and handcuffed him. Bethany rushed in to see Jo. She was relieved to see she was shaken but otherwise unhurt.

"You attract some interesting people," said Jo trying to make light of what had happened.

"I'm so glad you're all right," said Bethany. "I would never have forgiven myself if you'd been hurt."

"I'm ok."

"You know, he's done this before."

"I know now," said Jo.

"I'm so glad it's all over. We should celebrate but I don't feel like it. What about just having a quiet night with a bottle of wine?"

"Sounds good to me," said Jo.

That's what they did although they were a bit subdued. Bethany was just glad the whole affair was over. Now maybe she could get back to normal life.